duplicate

This book should be returned/renewed by the latest date shown above. Overdue items incur charges which prevent self-service renewals. Please contact the library.

Wandsworth Libraries
24 hour Renewal Hotline
01159 293388
www.wandsworth.gov.uk

Also by
Garth Edwards

For younger readers:
The Adventures of Titch & Mitch

For older readers:
THE THORN GATE TRILOGY

THE THORN GATE TRILOGY

BOOK THREE

HEROES OF MERCY HALL

by
Garth Edwards

with illustrations by
Max Stasyuk

INSIDE POCKET

Published in Great Britain by
Inside Pocket Publishing Limited

First published in Great Britain 2012
Text copyright © Garth Edwards 2011

The right of Garth Edwards to be identified as
the author of this work has been asserted
by him in accordance with the
Copyright, Designs and Patents Act 1988

Illustrations copyright © Inside Pocket Publishing Limited 2012
Cover image © Inside Pocket Publishing Limited 2012

A CIP catalogue record for this book is available from
the British Library

ISBN 978 0 9567122 6 4

Inside Pocket Publishing Limited Reg. No. 06580097

Printed and bound by CPI Group
(UK) Ltd, Croydon, CR0 4YY

www.insidepocket.co.uk

CONTENTS

I

THE CHIMNEY SWEEP

It was the incident with the chimney sweep that brought the strange world behind the hedge to its dramatic and unexpected conclusion...

As part of her spring cleaning routine, Mavis Minchcombe, the housekeeper, decided that the large chimney in the main hall needed to be swept clean, so a local sweep was sent for and duly arrived the very next day.

When Robert met him at the rear door of the house, he was quite taken by surprise. The man was large, with burly shoulders, a pronounced gait and walked with the aid of a stout cane. The most startling part of his appearance was his thick black hair, which covered his face and chin far more than it did the top of his head, leaving only puffy, red cheeks visible below his beady, coal-black eyes.

'Good day to you, young sir,' said the man, raising his hat and inclining his head slightly to look down at Robert. 'I wish to meet with the housekeeper, if I may.'

'And who might you be?' asked Robert quietly. He was the oldest boy in the orphanage and managed the business affairs of the place, though it was agreed that in domestic dealings with the outside

world, Mavis should take charge, so as not to raise any suspicions.

'My name is Black Mike, *chimeny* sweep of distinction,' replied the man, handing Robert a grubby, soot-stained card. Before Robert even had a chance to read it, the card was snatched back and tucked neatly into the sweep's breast pocket. 'I've come to clean your *chimenies*, as directed...'

As he spoke, he was joined on the steps by two other gaunt and blackened figures. One of them was a young man, tall and jumpy, with a twitch in his left eye, wearing a black shirt and trousers cut off at the knee and carrying a bundle of dusty rags. The other was a small boy, aged no more than seven, covered from head to toe in black soot, so that only the white's of his eyes were visible. Naked, apart from tight shorts, he was as thin as a pikestaff and shivered in the chill morning air; from cold or from fear, Robert could not be sure.

'Allow me to introduce my associates,' continued Black Mike, gesturing towards the new arrivals. 'This is my assistant, Puny Pete, a fine worker and an expert in *chimenies* of all shapes and sizes. And this little scrag is my climber. I forget his name.'

'Rufus...' muttered Puny Pete, under his breath, though Black Mike ignored him. Pete's eye twitched.

'If you would be so kind as to direct my team to the said *chimeny*, we'll get started,' said Black Mike in a commanding voice.

Robert hesitated, taken aback by the sight of a young boy looking so pathetic.

'Time is money, my man.' The big man emphasised his point by removing a watch from his waistcoat pocket and staring at it intently.

'Come this way then,' said Robert, reluctantly.

Inside the main hall, Robert gestured to the fireplace. 'There it is. How will you clean it?'

Black Mike stroked his bushy beard and pointed at the boy. 'This little scamp... what's your name boy?'

'Rufus...' Puny Pete muttered with an exasperated

sigh and another twitch of his eye.

'He's new, but a good brusher,' explained Black Mike. 'He climbs up the *chimeny* and when he gets to the top he comes down again, scrubbing and cleaning off the soot as he descends. Puny then collects the soot as it falls down and shovels it into a sack. Simple.'

'Isn't it dangerous for such a little child to climb up the chimney? What if he should fall or get stuck?' said Robert, concerned about the boy's welfare.

'It's the only way!' exclaimed Black Mike in a surprised voice. 'I won't fit up that *chimeny*, Puny here used to, but he grew too big. Now he's almost useless, but I keep him on to clear up the mess. That boy gets fed, sleeps on coal sacks in the cellar and I have him washed three times a year. Sometimes four, if I'm feeling generous. The parish are grateful I took him out of the poorhouse. He's good for nothing else, anyway... Now please, stand aside and let me get to work.'

Black Mike didn't actually do any of the work; he settled himself down in a chair at the back of the room and shouted orders to Puny. 'Poke him up the chimney! Go on, get moving, time is money. I can't sit around here all day!'

Puny tied a brush to the boy's waist, picked him up and squatted in the fireplace. He raised little Rufus over his shoulders and pushed him up the chimney. There was a squeal as the child disappeared and a great pall of soot descended to cover Puny and settle on the floor of the hall. Puny stepped back and covered the opening with an old sheet to keep the falling soot from clouding into the room.

Robert and some of the residents of Mercy Hall stood and watched with alarm. None of them had ever seen a chimney cleaned before and their concern for little Rufus made them edgy; they frowned at each other and glared at Puny and Black Mike.

After a few minutes the scrabbling noise made by Rufus stopped and a plaintive voice, full of terror, shouted down. 'I'm stuck!'

'Tarnation!' thundered Black Mike as he eased himself out of his chair. 'That useless little monkey is going to cost me money if he spends all day playing up there!' He lumbered across the room to the fireplace and pushed Puny out of the way.'

'Please help me!' called out Rufus in a faint voice.

'I'll help you all right,' roared Black Mike. 'I'll warm up your bottom! That'll get you to the top soon enough.' The angry man pulled a bundle of paper out of a deep pocket in his coat and stuffed it into the grate. Before anyone could stop him, he struck a match and set fire to it.

'NO!' Robert and the watching children all shouted together. Rushing forward they grabbed the burning paper with their bare hands and pulled it out of the grate.

'Don't you interfere with my business!' roared Black Mike and he pushed the children away.

Robert staggered backwards. Turning to Raffer and his twin sister, Agnes, he said, 'Go and fetch

Milly.' Then, standing tall, he placed himself between Black Mike and the chimney. White faced and trembling he stared up at the chimney sweep. 'You will remove yourself from this house immediately; I will have no cruelty here. You will not be sweeping this *chimeny*!'

Black Mike placed his hands on his hips and laughed. 'Good, then I'll take my money for a day's work and be on my way.'

'You will take nothing of the sort, sir! I am more likely to report you for cruelty to a child.'

Mike roared with laughter again. 'There is no such offence. That boy is my property and I do what I like with him. Now, out of my way and I'll warm up his bottom again. That'll shift him for sure.'

A shrill, icy voice cut through the room. 'Oh no you won't!'

Milly strode rapidly into the hall. She was twelve years old and quite skinny, but the power she had gained in the Rainbow Cave gave her enormous confidence. Her pretty, freckled face was set like stone as she approached the chimney sweep. Robert and the children knew of her powers and watched with bated breath as she joined them. They had seen her fight the Robes behind the hedge and knew what she was capable of.

'OUT,' she said in a controlled rage. 'Leave this house now. We have to help this boy get free.'

Black Mike stood with his hands on his hips and pulled himself up to his full height. 'And who is going to make me?' he snarled.

The children knew that one punch from Milly would send him grovelling to the floor, but they also knew it would mean her power would not be secret any more.

For a moment they all glared at Black Mike who sniggered and sneered at all of them. Then a low rumbling growl came from the doorway, announcing the arrival Drago. The large dog seemed to grow bigger as he walked stiff legged towards Black Mike. The children of Mercy Hall were being threatened and the dog knew it. He considered himself their protector and was getting very angry. The hairs on his back stood on end and his eyes glowed red as his rage grew. He walked slowly with his head lowered and when he snarled at Black Mike the chimney sweep saw huge glistening fangs.

The big man blustered and backed away from the angry dog. Drago just followed him slowly, snarling.

'All right, I'm going,' he called out, staring at the approaching dog as he retreated. 'But I want my property back. That boy is mine and you can't steal him from me. I'll have the Beak on you.'

Puny joined his boss and they edged slowly towards the exit, keeping as far away from Drago as possible. Finally they rushed out of the house and, climbing onto their horse and cart, headed off down the path.

Before they reached the gate, Black Mike pulled the horses to a halt.

'What are you doing?' asked Puny Pete.

'Waiting...' replied his surly boss.

'What for?'

'To get my property back!'

As soon as Black Mike and Puny Pete had left, the children rushed to the fireplace. Robert called up the chimney. 'Are you all right, Rufus?'

A coughing and choking noise indicated that Rufus was still alive, but the smoke from Black Mike's burning paper had made his condition much worse.

'We need to do something quickly!' said Milly, looking at the others in desperation. 'Does anyone know how to get him down?'

'I do,' said a quiet voice.

They all stared at Digby. He was the housekeeper's son and about the same size as Rufus. 'I can go down the chimney with a rope. If I can tie it around Rufus, then you lot can pull us both out.'

'You can get to the roof through the attic,' said Raffer. 'It's dangerous up there, and there are lots of chimneys, but I know which is which.'

'Then lead us to it!' said Robert.

'I know where there's a long rope,' added Agnes.

'Fetch it! Singer, tell Mrs Minchcombe to put some water on and get the bath tub ready.'

The children raced out, their feet pounding on the stairs in a rush towards the attic.

'Elspeth,' Robert called back the smallest girl. 'You stay here and keep talking to Rufus. Keep him calm. Tell him we'll get him out very soon.'

'I will,' replied the little girl firmly. As Elspeth

took up position by the grate, Robert ran to join the others.

Once they had located the right chimney, Digby stripped down to his underwear and climbed up to the rim. He gulped as he looked down into the darkness.

'It's a long way down,' said Tod, the tall, lanky Rocket Boy from the land beyond the thorn hedge, who had climbed up with him. He looked down into the darkness, clutching the end of the rope handed to him by Agnes. 'A very long way down...'

'I'd better get going then,' said Digby, flashing Tod a wide grin.

Tod tied the rope around Digby's waist, leaving a long end for Digby to tie around Rufus. Bracing himself against the chimney, Tod prepared to take the strain. Digby wasted no time, although his teeth were chattering with fear and his legs felt weak at the prospect of descending down the narrow space. Taking a deep breath, the determined boy wriggled head first into the chimney.

Tod lowered the rope slowly. Digby found that the further down he went the wider the chimney became until he saw a bend in front of him. This was the point where Rufus had got stuck. The light had almost disappeared but Digby could just see Rufus jammed half way round the bend.

Digby dangled the end of the rope down to the trapped boy.

'Can you tie the rope around your waist?' he

called.

There was a choking noise as the poor stuck boy tried to reply. As Digby's eyes got used to the dark, he realised that so much soot had covered Rufus that he couldn't speak and could hardly move.

Digby tried again. 'Can you raise your hands over your head?' he asked, conscious that soot was still falling down and slowly covering him as well.

At first there was no response, then slowly one hand was lifted upwards. After some scratching and wriggling, the other one was raised as well.

'Lower me down a bit further!' shouted Digby. Carefully, Tod let out a little more rope.

'Stop!' Digby called out. He could reach Rufus's raised hands now and, stretching out, tied the end of the rope as tightly as he could around them. Then, closing his eyes, he called up to those above.

'PULL US UP!' As the first tug jolted him against the side of the chimney, he added, 'CAREFULLY!'

It was hard enough work pulling Digby back up the chimney, but Tod managed to raise him a little way; then the rope tightened around the hands of Rufus and he started to move as well, but only a few inches. The extra weight was too much for Tod alone. Behind him, other hands gripped the rope to help take the weight.

'All together now!' shouted George, who stood right behind Tod.

'Don't jerk it!' shouted Sam, the next in line. 'Pull gently!'

'One, two, three … heave!' cried Tod, and with

the extra strength on the rope, Rufus broke free from the bend in the chimney. The boys carried on pulling. Digby rose backwards up the chimney scraping more soot from the walls as he went. Rufus came up with him and dislodged more and more of the soot which cascaded down to the grate below.

Inch by inch they rose, until Digby's feet began to appear. Hands grabbed at his ankles and pulled him gently out of the chimney. He was covered in soot and the children cheered as they flapped and scraped the black dust off him. Digby choked and gasped for breath but insisted he was all right. Then everyone turned to help Tod drag Rufus over the edge of the chimney. The little sweep couldn't open his eyes or speak but lay on the slates in a distressed state, choking and trying to breathe.

'We need to get him downstairs, fast!' said George.

'Allow me,' said Sam, stepping up and lifting the boy into his arms. He then ran with him down the stairs, taking the steps two at a time, until he reached the kitchen where an anxious Mavis Minchcombe waited with a bucket of hot water and a cloth.

'You poor creature,' tutted the housekeeper as she rinsed the soot off the skinny boy and then set to work with a bar of soap.

Moments later, Digby appeared in the doorway, black as night.

'Goodness me,' she shouted in alarm as she realised the black creature in front of her was her own son.'

'I'm all right, Ma!' he said with a black-faced grin that went from ear to ear.

When all the children eventually arrived back from the roof they crowded round Digby, hailing him as a hero and vowing that there would be no cruelty to children in Mercy Hall.

Another black figure appeared at the door.

'Elspeth!' cried Robert. 'What happened to you?'

'I was talking to Rufus, when a whole pile of soot landed on me.' The bewildered girl said, spitting soot from her mouth. 'It was horrible...'

Soon the three of them were cleaned up and dressed in fresh clothes. Rufus was especially pleased; he couldn't remember the last time he'd actually worn a clean shirt.

'This is so kind of you. I should like to stay here for ever!' he said in a sad little voice, knowing Black Mike would be back for him soon enough.

'And so you shall!' exclaimed Mavis Minchcombe. 'If I see that wicked scoundrel again, I'll give him a piece of my mind.' She carried on fussing over the two little boys with tears running down her cheeks.

'We need a plan,' said Robert. 'Black Mike will want Rufus back, and if we don't return him, then he's sure to go to the magistrate.'

'But we won't have a problem if Rufus runs away from Black Mike and gets back here without anyone knowing,' suggested George.

'Except that Black Mike could claim him back if he ever found out,' added Milly.

'I don't think Black Mike would recognise him,' said George thoughtfully, as he looked at the boy. 'He's only ever seen him covered in soot. Now look at him! He looks completely different when he's clean. I think we should cover his face with soot again. This time as a disguise, then hand him back to Black Mike. As soon as the horse and cart get back to Mike's workplace, Rufus can run away.'

'But Puny will easily catch me,' said Rufus, choking back tears at the thought of being caught and made to clean chimneys again.

'Not if the fastest runner in the world is waiting round the corner,' said George, turning to look at Sam.

'Of course,' cried Sam. 'Don't worry Rufus, I'll be waiting for you. Even with you on my back, I can outpace Puny and Black Mike, and their cart.'

The children reassured Rufus that Sam was telling the truth. Since gaining his gift in the Rainbow Cave, Sam could run faster than any horse, or even a whole team of horses. Black Mike's nag was no match for him.

Though the little boy looked doubtful, he nodded his head slowly to show he agreed with the plan.

'You must wait until you get back to Mike's yard before you run away,' said George. 'We want Black Mike to look for you in town and not here,' he added.

Rufus had recovered well, but when he was covered in soot again and returned to the big chimney sweep, he pretended to be weak and needed to be carried to the horse and cart waiting for him.

Black Mike snorted in triumph as Puny dumped the boy into the back of the cart.

'Nice to have you back,' he said, cracking his whip at the horse. The cart jerked slowly forward and trundled steadily down the drive.

As soon as the cart was out of sight, Sam gave chase, keeping a steady distance behind, making sure not to be spotted by Black Mike or Puny. Whenever people came in sight, Sam would slow his pace, so as not to draw attention to his incredible speed. It was vital that all special powers remain secret at all times.

Black Mike's workplace was a dusty yard adjoining a crumbling house on the outskirts of Erringford. Its dark windows and peeling paint offered little in the way of welcome. When the horse and cart came to a stop, Sam was right behind, crouching in the shadows of a nearby wall. The only person who knew he was there was Rufus. From his position in the back of the cart he had watched Sam jogging behind them all the way. Sam winked at Rufus and motioned to him to choose his moment well. Rufus nodded in reply to show he understood.

Puny had climbed down from the front of the cart and was swinging open the wooden gates to the yard. They moved with a creaking groan, as though unwilling to shift at all. Black Mike remained seated, scratching the back of his neck and muttering something about *chimenies*.

Seeing the time was right, Rufus steadily crawled over the black, grubby sacks and slid himself down off the back of the cart. As his feet hit the ground, Black Mike turned.

'Where do you think you're going?' he cried.

With a quick backward glance at Black Mike and Puny, the terrified little boy launched himself into a sprint.

'Come back!' roared Black Mike. 'Puny, get that boy back here!'

Though thin and wiry, Puny could move fast. He followed Rufus round the side of the wall but came to a sudden stop, his eyes darting from left to right and twitching like mad. There was no sign of the little boy, only an old lady walking slowly towards them, pulling her shawl tight around her neck.

'Sudden wind...' she mumbled, and moved on.

Black Mike joined Puny. Together they looked in bewilderment at the empty street.

'Search everywhere,' ordered Black Mike. 'He must have climbed over the wall or dodged into a doorway.'

'That boy couldn't climb the wall, and all the doors are shut,' objected Puny, staring down the street. 'He's just disappeared.'

Sam was already crouched on the ground like a sprinter when Rufus shot round the corner and jumped straight onto his back. The little boy wrapped his arms tight around Sam's neck and held on for dear life. It was just as well. Sam took off like a sprinter and after a few strides was moving like a rocket. His feet skimmed the ground and a passer-by would have seen only a blur as he gathered speed. The little old lady didn't even see him as he passed her; she just felt a blast of wind from his slipstream, making her stumble and nearly lose her shawl.

Sam made his way cross country. Once he was sure there was no pursuit, he slowed down to a more relaxed jog.

'Golly!' said Rufus, as they reached the grounds of Mercy Hall. 'I won't forget this. You must be the fastest runner in the world! Can we go round again?'

'Maybe later,' chuckled Sam. 'Right now, you need another wash.'

2

THE BROTHERS TWIST

Some time after rescuing Rufus from Black Mike's clutches, the circus came to town.

A large crowd gathered at the newly built Erringford railway station to await the arrival of *The Brothers Twist Funtime Circus*. Bunting was

draped across the platforms and brightly coloured flags fluttered from high poles. It was just after school and children from all over town, including those from Mercy Hall, watched open-mouthed as the giant train pulled in, puffing and blowing steam like some mythical dragon.

Truck doors slid open, and soon the platform was a bustling throng: jugglers, clowns, acrobats and dancers, all mingling with astonished townsfolk, while lions, tigers, and even an elephant, were led to the nearby field where a massive tent had already been erected.

That evening Robert announced that he had purchased tickets for the Saturday performance of the circus. The children cheered and clapped at the news and counted the passing days with barely contained excitement.

The circus performed twice a day for the people of the district and the residents of Mercy Hall were there in force on Saturday afternoon. It was a great occasion. None of the children had ever seen tigers jumping through hoops or bareback riders standing on horses as they galloped round the circus ring.

The clowns were hugely popular and had the children in fits of laughter as they tumbled and bounced around the giant arena. A high wire act made everyone hold their breath as a team of girls holding poles tiptoed along a tight wire stretched over the circus ring. Immediately after them, the necks of the youngsters in the audience were strained

upwards again when the flying trapeze artists swung into action with a dazzling performance of daring somersaults and leaps, with nothing to catch them should they fall. And the sight of the elephant parading around had them all aghast; they had never seen an animal so enormous.

It was an exhausted but happy crowd of children who made their way home to Mercy Hall that day. Even the following day they were still talking about it in breathless tones. A number of them were determined to become circus performers. But the mood changed at lunchtime, when they discovered that Digby was missing.

The housekeeper's son, being a small boy with a big appetite, never missed lunch. His mother hurried to his room to look for him, in a flurry of anxiety.

When she returned a few minutes later, her face was white and her lips quivered. 'His bed has not been slept in!' she gasped and then had to sit down.

'Everybody search the house and grounds immediately!' called Robert. With a clatter of chairs everybody rushed outside and upstairs. For the rest of the day they looked high and low but to no avail; Digby remained missing.

Monday lessons were postponed as the search was widened, with some of the older children heading into town to see if they could discover any news of Digby's whereabouts. Towards evening, Raffer and Agnes came storming into the hall, breathless but excited.

Raffer spoke hurriedly. 'I met a boy called Billy Bowman. He said he thought he saw a small boy feeding the chimpanzees at the circus this afternoon. He was exploring round the back of the tent before the evening show started. He only got a glimpse and he couldn't be sure because he was shooed away by the white faced clown.'

'What makes him think it was Digby?' asked Robert.

Agnes shrugged. 'Nothing really. He was only trying to help.'

Robert folded his arms and settled his face into a deep frown. 'Where can he have got to?'

'What about Black Mike?' said Milly with a start. 'It's two weeks since we took Rufus away from him. If he hasn't found a replacement, he might have taken Digby instead. He's about the same size.'

Robert shook his head.

'I don't think Black Mike could sneak into Mercy Hall and kidnap Digby without Drago or any of us seeing him,' he said doubtfully. 'Anyway his bed wasn't slept in, so he must have disappeared before bedtime.'

'If he did go back to the circus in the evening, then Black Mike could have spotted him,' added Milly.

At that moment George hurried in looking anxious. 'I was searching the path by the hedge. Someone has stuck a post in the ground right where the hedge can be opened,' he said.

Only the children who had been through the hedge to the strange land beyond knew the secret of how and where to make it open and this news stopped all conversation.

'That means that someone has come out from behind the hedge and marked the spot so they can return,' said Milly slowly. A shiver ran down her spine as she wondered which of the creatures who lived there could have entered their world.

'I pulled up the post and got rid of it,' said George. 'Whoever is here will have to stay here. Any sign of Digby?'

Several heads shook sadly. Others looked down.

'A possible sighting at the circus,' said Robert. 'Not very much to go on.'

'We should follow them up just in case,' said George.

'I think Charlie and Singer should track down

the circus,' decided Robert. 'Charlie can talk to the animals and Singer can become invisible, which might be a great help.

'I'll go as well!' came a shrill voice from above them. It was Batty, the talking Tick-Tock bird who was perched on a rafter. She looked like a hamster with bat-like wings and could talk because she had been through the Rainbow Cave.

'All right,' said Robert looking up. 'But if you do, you must not let people hear you talking. It would cause enormous problems if word got out that we have a talking bird at Mercy Hall. It's a secret and we have to keep it that way.'

'Of course I won't talk. Nobody listens to me anyway. I'm a very clever Tick-Tock bird and I know lots of things, but everyone tells me to shush whenever I speak.' The indignant bird flew down to rest on Charlie's shoulder. 'I'm going to the circus to find Digby,' she added emphatically.

'I will go with Milly to visit Black Mike,' continued Robert. 'George, you'd best stay here and keep an eye on the hedge. If someone came through, they may try to get back. We need to catch them!'

George nodded. 'Righto.'

Looking around the room, Robert spotted Drago lying by the door with his head resting on his paws and watching the proceedings. He was also under strict orders that he didn't talk in front of strangers.

'Drago,' said Robert. 'Please make sure that no harm comes to the children while we are away.'

'Of course I will,' Drago said in his gruff voice.

3

BLACK MIKE AGAIN

It was the following morning before the investigations could start.

Robert and Milly were first to leave. They had decided on the direct approach and the determined look on Milly's face suggested the investigation would be very thorough indeed. They reached Erringford and soon found the dingy yard with the wooden gates. The scruffy building next to the yard had a door that was half open and hanging off its hinges but there was nobody to be seen.

Robert squeezed past the broken door and called out. 'Is anyone there?'

Milly stood behind him, looking around the room. There was dirt and soot everywhere and piles of sacks lay on the ground. Milly wrinkled her nose in distaste, then stared hard at some sacks in front of her. She thought one of them had moved. She nudged Robert and pointed at the sack. It moved again and slowly a small head poked out from underneath. It was a young boy with a black, sooty face, looking much like Rufus when he had first appeared. He stared back at them with wide, fearful eyes, then he pointed to another door across the room. 'Through that door,' he said in a quavering voice.

'What are you doing down there?' asked Milly in surprise.

'I sleep here,' said the boy.

'And your name?' asked Robert.

'Bruno.'

'What's going on out there?' roared a voice from behind the door. They recognised it at once as Black Mike's.

Robert looked down at Milly standing beside him. The little girl gave him a push. 'Go on, if Digby is here we have to find him!'

Tentatively, Robert pushed the door open and walked into the room, Milly following. Black Mike was sitting behind a makeshift desk which consisted of a large plank of wood stretched across two upright barrels. On the desk were a few small piles of copper coins. The sweep had been counting his earnings.

'You again,' sneered Black Mike, 'the snooty boy from the orphanage. Is that dog with you?' The man's eyes narrowed as he looked behind them.

'No, we don't need a dog to talk to you,' said Robert. He felt very nervous and was relieved to know that Milly was with him. The skinny little girl was trying hard to smile at the big sweep.

'We are looking for one of our boys. Digby is his name,' he said, 'and we have reason to believe you have taken him to replace poor Rufus, who we hear has run away from you.'

'That's my new boy out there,' said Mike, waving a thick-fingered hand towards the door. 'I forget his name, but I'm sure it's not Digby! Anyway, it's none of your business who I have as my climber!' His voice rose to a roar and he stood up, leaning on the desk, which wobbled underneath him. 'Keep your nose out of my affairs!' Then, flashing a grim smile, he sat back down and added, in softer tones, 'But I am glad you have come here, because you owe me for a day's work and now I can collect my due. I hope you have brought money with you because my services do not come cheap to those who give me grief!'

Standing again, he crossed the room and shut the door.

'The trouble you have caused me will be very expensive indeed.'

Facing the two children, he sneered and held out his hand. 'You're not going anywhere until I've finished with you. Come on, give me all you have, and I think I'll take those fancy clothes as well.'

Robert stepped back. 'Go on Milly. He's not going to be reasonable.'

The little girl stood her ground. As Black Mike approached, he swung his arm to push her out of the way. But Milly's hand reached up, and stopped the arm mid-swing.

'What the..?' said Black Mike, trying to move his arm and finding he couldn't.

'We want to know what you did with Digby?' asked Robert.

Black Mike tried to pull his arm away, but a small twist from Milly had him crumbling to his knees. He peered sideways at Milly with a look of utter disbelief on his face.

'I'll teach you a lesson you won't forget, little girl!' he spluttered and grabbed at Milly's leg. The large, meaty fingers wrapped around her ankle and squeezed tight. The big man heaved to bring the girl down. But, to his surprise, Milly's leg stayed firmly put. She was too strong to be moved.

Instead she reached out and took hold of his waist band with one hand and his collar with the other. With a great heave she lifted the big man off the ground and carried him over her head to his desk, where she sat him on the plank and stepped back. The desk groaned and tilted. The coins clattered and some of them fell to the floor. Black Mike grabbed the desk with trembling hands.

'What... what are you?' he stammered. 'Who are you? You're not a normal child!'

Robert stepped forward. 'I'm very sorry to have to use force,' he said politely. 'But we need some answers. If we don't get them, I'm afraid my companion may have to be a little less gentle with you.'

'I don't want any more trouble with you lot. I haven't got your lad.' Black Mike looked warily at them. 'Honest!'

'But I think you know where he is,' persisted Robert.

'No, I don't,' Black Mike's jaw trembled and he looked at Milly with fear in his eyes. 'I have another climber and he ain't called Digby.'

Robert had an idea. 'Bring that boy in here,' he said to Milly.

Milly fetched the soot covered boy into the room, holding him gently by the hand. Bruno stared at Black Mike sitting on the desk and shrank back in fear.

'Don't be frightened, Bruno,' said Milly gently. 'He's really a big old softy. He wants you to tell us where you came from and whether you have ever met a boy called Digby?'

'I don't know where I come from, but I was in

the poorhouse in Manchester and they gave me to a man called Mr Benjamin Smutt to train as a sweep.' The boy covered his face in his hands and started to cry. 'I don't want to be a sweep and I don't like it here.'

'How old are you?' asked Milly.

'I think I'm six,' replied Bruno, peeping at her through his fingers.

'How did you get here?'

'Mr Mike swopped me for the boy you mentioned... Digby.'

'He's lying!' said Black Mike and he tried to get off the desk.

Milly whirled round, pushed him back, then waved a small finger in front of his nose.

'My good man,' said Robert in his usual polite way. 'I really do advise you to tell us about Digby. Unless of course, you wish to experience further... grief?'

Black Mike glowered.

Robert was rapidly losing patience with the sweep. He wanted answers. Stepping back, he looked at Milly and gave her a nod. Before she could even step forward, Black Mike raised his hands in defence.

'No, no, no, I'll tell you!' Black Mike spluttered. 'Just keep her away from me.'

'Mind you tell the truth now!' said Milly scowling.

'The clown in the circus, Happy Harry. He watches out for orphans and the like, then takes them to sell on to factories and sweeps and whoever will buy them. He told me he had an orphan nobody wanted, so I bought him. I needed a new climber. Last one went missing, didn't he?'

'You can't *buy* children!' said Robert aghast.

Black Mike sneered. 'Really? Then I paid him a finder's fee. What's the difference?'

'Where is Digby now?' asked Milly. 'What have you done to him?'

'It turned out he came from an orphanage all right, but he ain't an orphan. His ma works there, don't she? Too risky to keep him here, I thinks, so I swopped him for another in Little Amberwell. Cost me a packet, too,' he grumbled.

'The name please,' demanded Robert. 'The sweep in Little Amberwell.'

'Benny Smutt.'

Robert and Milly were relieved to have found out what had happened to Digby but were concerned that he was still in danger. Little Amberwell was too far away to visit that day and they were anxious to get Bruno safely back to Mercy Hall. They certainly had no intention of leaving him with this cruel master.

'Mr Mike,' said Robert turning to the big sweep, still perched on the edge of his desk looking pale and fearful. 'I am going to give you some important investment advice. I suggest you listen carefully. There have of late been some developments in the world of chimney sweeping which eliminate the need for young boys to be used as climbers. These consist of mechanical devices which make use of brushes, ropes and pulleys and enable honourable and efficient sweeps to clean chimneys without the help of children. I recommend you invest in this new equipment in the very near future.'

'Kids are cheaper,' grumbled Black Mike.

'No, they are not,' said Robert sternly. 'Because we are taking Bruno away with us and if you acquire another replacement, we will do the same thing again. I promise you we will take every single child you get. That, my man, will be a lot more expensive, so good day to you and I hope we have no cause to ever meet again. I would hate to cause you any further *grief.*'

As they left, Puny stumbled in, his left eye twitching as usual.

'You all right, boss?' he asked, seeing his master still clinging to the uncertain desk.

'Puny?' asked Black Mike. 'What's a *pulley*?'

4

STRANGE HAPPENINGS AT FUNTIME CIRCUS

Tracking down the circus would take some time. The big tent had been pulled down and all the circus performers and their animals were gone. They had boarded the train and moved on to their next location.

As there could be a long journey ahead of them, Charlie and Singer packed a rucksack with supplies and set off later in the morning for the railway station. On arrival, Singer enquired politely as to the whereabouts of the circus.

'It's gone to Livingham, the next stop down the line,' said the clerk at the station with a tut. He was a bright young man in a shiny new uniform of deep blue with red piping around the collar and cuffs. 'All of them have gone, including the smelly animals, and I hope they don't come back for a long time. You should see the mess in our carriages.' He tutted some more, then added, 'Can I help you?'

'Yes, indeed you can. We would like two tickets for the next train to Livingham.'

'Oh dear,' said the clerk, narrowing his eyes. 'That train leaves in half an hour and it's fully booked. I'm sorry, but there is only one ticket left.'

'We'll take it,' said Charlie, with a wink at Singer. 'I'll go on my own,' he added for the benefit of the clerk.

Clutching the ticket, Charlie and Singer waited on the busy station platform. 'I shall make myself scarce,' said Singer, giving Charlie a nudge. 'See you on the train.'

'I hope it's not too crowded,' he replied. Singer smiled.

'Don't worry. I'm sure I can squeeze in somewhere.' Then she added with a wink, 'I'm quite excited. I've never been on a train before.'

A long piercing whistle announced the arrival of the train. People stepped back from the edge as it pulled up alongside the platform with a squeal of brakes and a billowing cloud of steam. Singer saw her chance to use her power; she slipped away and became invisible.

Quick and nimble, Charlie was one of the first into the carriage and sat himself down next to the window. It might only be a short journey, but Charlie was also excited at being on a train and wanted to see the landscape rushing by. As other people crowded into the carriage, he hoped for a sign that Singer was amongst them. But as the whistle blew and the train pulled out, he had no idea if she was even on it.

'Where are you?' whispered Charlie quietly. There was no reply. He stretched his arms and pretended to yawn, hoping he would be able to touch her, but he couldn't feel anything.

'Don't fidget, boy!' said a grumpy old man in the

neighbouring seat. 'You're giving me jitters!'

Charlie glowered, but could do nothing. Instead, he glued his eyes to the window and watched the fields, houses and trees flash by. He laughed out loud when a herd of cows, alarmed by the noise and steam from the train, took fright and stampeded across a field. Though he enjoyed the journey, he had a nagging worry that maybe Singer had been left behind. At least he knew Batty was with him, though she had opted to fly, not liking the idea of being stuck in a moving carriage.

Ten minutes later the driver blew the train's whistle again and it slowed down for the approach to the station at Livingham. The carriage came to a juddering halt. Charlie took his time getting off, hoping for some sign of Singer, but as the train started off again and chugged out of the station, he found himself standing alone on the platform. With a deep sigh, he wondered what to do next.

'Hand in your ticket,' said a familiar voice right behind him.

'Where have you *been*?' asked Charlie, whirling round to look for Singer.

'Shh! People will think you're talking to yourself! I can't become visible yet because I haven't got a ticket.'

Once they were outside the station and on their own, Singer came back into view and explained. 'I need plenty of space to be invisible. All those people pushing and shoving about - it didn't look safe, so

39

I ran down the platform and sneaked in with the driver on the engine.'

'You lucky egg!' exclaimed Charlie. 'I'd love to be in the cab with the driver. What was it like?'

'Smelly, noisy, dirty and very hot,' she replied, unimpressed. 'I didn't realise I was standing next to the whistle until the driver pulled the chain. I thought my head would explode.' Rubbing her still sore ears, she added, 'I don't think I like trains very much.'

A tick-tock sound announced the arrival of an exhausted Batty.

'Well,' she said through heavy puffs. 'That was hard work.'

'Come on,' said Charlie, getting to his feet. 'Let's go and find the circus.'

'What!' gasped Batty. 'But I've only just arrived...'

By the time Singer and Charlie found the circus, the performers and their helpers were preparing for the evening performance.

A fence had been put up around the great tent which included the area where the animals were kept. The two children walked alongside it but could not find a way in. Batty, once she got her breath back, had flown on ahead to scout the area. Charlie spotted her sitting on the highest pole at the top of the great tent. Suddenly a band started up and the noise made by all the cheering children inside the tent grew to a cacophonous roar.

'Let's watch the performance,' suggested Charlie.

'We can then sneak off and hide somewhere. When the show is over, we'll be inside the fence.'

'And if Digby is in there, we might see him,' added Singer.

They hurried to the entrance and joined the long queue for tickets. Once inside, Charlie spotted some seats near the tunnel where all the performers and the animals trooped in and out of the arena. They quickly scrambled over to them and sat down.

The first performers were the clowns led by Happy Harry. He was a clown with a painted white face. Black circles were painted round his mouth and eyes and he wore a red and white striped jump suit with white lace frills around his neck and wrists. Although he was dressed to make children laugh, some of the smaller ones were shy and preferred to hide behind their parents. A model train, a little like the one they had arrived on, puffed around the edge of the ring, steam billowing out of its chimney. The clowns would jump on the carriages, then fall off, much to everyone's great amusement. Balloons filled with water were thrown into the audience to be met with screams of laughter as they burst open, drenching anyone nearby.

Although Charlie and Singer laughed at the antics, they also kept their sharp eyes open for any sign of Digby.

Lions ran down the tunnel next to them and out into a great wire cage, where they jumped through hoops and pretended to fight with their trainers. All the children cheered loudly and some of them were invited into the cage to stroke the big beasts.

Four chimpanzees had a tea party, which everyone thought was hilarious, as the animals were dressed up like humans in trousers or skirts and very smart hats. They could do backward somersaults and tumble forwards at great speed. But if they got too near the spectators the trainer, a narrow faced man who never smiled, would crack a whip at the offending chimp and send him screaming back to his fellows. This made the spectators laugh even louder.

The chimps received a loud round of applause at the end of their act and were made to bow as they backed out of the arena. As they passed Charlie, he could hear them jabbering away to each other and understood every word perfectly.

'One of those children offered me a sweet,' said the smallest chimp, 'and that Nasty Norman cracked the whip at me. He's horrid. I don't like this circus. I want to go home.'

'One day, we'll find a way,' said the largest chimp.

Twisting round in his seat he called after the departing animals. 'I'll come and talk to you later, watch out for me!'

Immediately all four of the chimps stopped and turned to face him. Their mouths were wide open with surprise. As they were too far away to talk properly, Charlie waved and smiled at them.

Just then, Nasty Norman walked past and glared at Charlie. Charlie smiled, but the trainer seemed in no mood to be pleasant. Instead, he drew back his whip and whistled the end of it over the heads of the chimps, before bringing it back with a fearsome crack. The chimps turned and fled from the arena and out of sight.

Some of the people around Charlie smiled at him, they had heard him jabbering at the chimps and thought he was pretending to be like them. Singer, however clutched at his arm. 'Are you talking to them?' she hissed in his ear.

'Yes, I said I would talk to them later. We have to hide somewhere after the show and then go and look for them. They might have some information about Digby.'

'*You'll* have to hide,' she corrected him with a smile. '*I* can disappear, then go and have a look around.'

At the end of the show, after all the acrobats, clowns, animal trainers and trapeze artists had done their final circuit of the ring, and the audience had clapped and cheered themselves hoarse, all the circus folk left the arena and the audience joined the queue to leave the big tent.

Charlie and Singer lingered behind. When nobody was looking, Singer slipped into the shadows and disappeared.

Charlie bent down and pretended to tie his shoe before wriggling down into the space underneath the seating. Singer also found a way down under the seats and took hold of Charlie's hand to let him know she had joined him. They found some old

sacks and Charlie hid underneath them while Singer sat next to him with her back against the tent.

'When all the people have gone,' she whispered, 'I'll go and find out where the chimps are, then I'll come and get you. Let's hope they have seen Digby.'

'I need a disguise,' said Charlie in a worried voice. 'Now all the people have gone, a child wandering around by himself is bound to attract attention.'

'Have a look over there,' suggested Singer, pointing Charlie's hand in the direction of a number of wicker baskets stacked together in a corner. There was plenty of space in the area beneath the rows of seats and the circus workers used it to store everything that was not needed during the performance. 'You may find a costume of some sort. Try to blend in...'

Soon, the chatter of children's voices and the

laughter of adults died down as the last audience members left the tent. Singer announced that she would go and explore and be as quick as she could.

While she was gone, Charlie rummaged through the crates. Inside he found an assortment of clothes used by the clowns for their shows; with all that water flying around, a great number of costume changes were needed. As there were two dwarves among the troop of clowns, he was hoping to find some of their clothes, as they were more likely to fit him. At the very bottom he found a pair of short, baggy, black trousers, a red shirt and a false beard. 'Just the job,' he thought. 'I won't be a child wandering around; I'll be a small clown.'

He dressed in the trousers and shirt and was struggling to fit on the beard when he heard Singer's voice behind him. 'Let me do that,' she said. Taking the false beard, she hooked the wires over his ears. 'There you are! A perfect fit and a brilliant disguise.'

'Did you find anything?' he asked, scratching his chin. The disguise may have been brilliant, but it wasn't comfortable.

'Yes, I've found the cage where the chimps are kept,' she replied. 'They're jabbering amongst themselves a lot. I think they got an enormous surprise when you spoke to them.'

'Come on then, take my hand and lead me to them.'

Squeezing out from behind the seats, Charlie marched boldly alongside Singer. Although they passed many of the circus workers, none of them paid any attention to him. Most of them were too exhausted after a hard day's work to think anything odd of a small clown. Singer led him straight to a cage in the middle of the animal area and, after looking carefully around to see if anyone was watching, said, 'Be visible!'.

As they approached, four chimpanzee faces stopped their jabbering and turned to look at them with acute interest. Their long fingers gripped the bars of the cage tightly, and their heads tilted from left to right as they tried to make sense of these strange children before them.

'Hello there,' jabbered Charlie in a half whisper, and pulling down his beard, he added, 'Look, it's me! I'm Charlie. I called out to you when you were leaving the circus ring.'

All of the chimps started talking together in a flurry of excitement. 'Quiet!' said Charlie. 'One at a time, please. First of all, what are your names?'

'Me Mo,' said the largest chimp and, waving an arm at the chimp next to him, he added, 'This Flo, them Bee and Bo. Children.'

Charlie translated for the benefit of Singer.

'What lovely names,' said Singer smiling at the chimps. 'Mo, Flo, Bee and Bo.'

'Never met people speak chimp,' said Flo. 'How know?'

'It's a long story,' replied Charlie. 'Let's just say it's a gift. We are looking for a small boy named Digby. He may have joined the circus recently, or he may be kept as a prisoner somewhere. Have any of you seen him?'

The four chimps stared at each other for a while and then each one slowly shook its head. 'Sorry,' said Mo and looked sadly at him. 'Know no Digby...'

But then the little chimp, who wore a frock, began to jump back and forth saying, 'What about red caravan? Might be red caravan!'

'Red caravan?' asked Charlie. 'What's in there?'

'Bad place,' said Mo. 'Happy Harry's red caravan. We hear noises from red caravan. None go in but Harry. Bad place...'

'And Puffy Face,' chipped in Flo. 'Bring animals in sacks. Bad man.'

'Did you see any of them?' asked Charlie.

'No, but Puffy Face wild. Big man, gone wild. Bad man...' Flo shuddered as she remembered the moment.

Charlie translated for Singer who said, 'We have to check inside that caravan. Ask them where it is.'

Before Charlie could say anything, a loud voice called out from behind them. 'Ah, I've got you at last!'

The chimps were so surprised they jumped about a foot off the ground at the sudden interruption and darted to the back of their cage. Singer and Charlie whirled round in shock, amazed that anyone could get so close without being seen. But it was only Batty. She had glided silently down to perch on the lion's cage just behind them. 'Where have you been and what's going on?' she said. 'What sort of weird animals are those hairy monsters you are talking to?'

'Batty!' exclaimed Singer in relief. 'Don't do that! Don't sneak up on us and frighten us like that.'

Batty chortled and stretched her wings so they clicked. 'Excuse me, but there's nobody around. I checked first.'

'Don't be alarmed,' said Charlie to the chimps. 'It's only our friend, Batty. She's helping us to find Digby. She's a very annoying bird who never stops talking, but she's a good friend.'

'And I know where the red caravan is!' added Batty.

'Then let's check it out,' said Charlie. 'Thank you for your help.' He started to walk away.

The chimps just stared at Batty in amazement and slowly approached the front of their cage again. Mo pointed a finger at Batty and jabbered suddenly.

The lion, in the cage that Batty was perched on, had come slowly out from the shadows behind her. His head was down and his eyes glistened like diamonds. The deadly animal moved quietly into the moonlight, staring intently up at the bird who had the audacity to sit on the top of *his* cage.

Charlie realised that Mo was warning Batty of the impending danger. 'Batty! Move!' he shouted.

'I shall move when I'm good and ready.' Batty had decided she was not going to take any more orders.

As she spoke, a huge paw, with claws extended, made a lightning strike at her. Singer screamed and lurched towards Batty. The sudden movement frightened the bird, who leapt off her perch, screeching as she went. The sharp claws swept through the bars of the cage and through the air where Batty had been sitting. Luckily, all they could grasp was a single tail feather. The lion roared with frustration at missing the bird and swung his paw through the bars of the cage again as if challenging someone to come near. They all leapt back in alarm.

The lion roared again; any minute somebody might come to investigate. Hurriedly, Charlie waved farewell to the chimps and he and Singer turned to run away.

'Stop!' cried Flo, calling after them. 'Please open cage before you go.'

Charlie stopped and, with a nervous look at the growling lion, he returned to help the chimps.

'Where is the key?' he asked, anxious to be away from the lion's cage and terrified lest someone appear at any moment.

'On hook by door of green caravan,' said Flo, pointing to an old green caravan that looked like a broken down shed on wheels. 'Don't worry, Nasty Norman not there. Hook inside. Be quick! We run when others sleep.' All the chimps were holding onto the bars of their cage and bouncing up and down with excitement.

Charlie raced over to the caravan. Throwing caution to the wind, he opened the door. Immediately, he saw a set of keys on a hook. He grabbed them and returned to the chimps. Mo snatched them out of his hand and all four of them rushed to the back of their cage and started jabbering together in low voices.

Batty was very unhappy. Although most of her body was covered in fur which made her look a lot like a hamster when sitting quietly, she had a set of tail feathers which she used to steer when in flight. It was the loss of a feather that caused her distress.

'That stupid cat is a vicious evil monster and needs to be taught a lesson. How can a Tick-Tock bird fly properly without its feathers,' she screeched loudly. All thought of caution had gone and the angry bird would not be consoled. She fluttered wildly above them spluttering and tick-tocking furiously.

The bad-tempered lion retreated to the back of its cage and Batty flew down and perched on the top of its cage again. Poking her head down through the bars she screeched as loudly as she could at the lion. 'I'll be back, you overweight pussy cat! You'll pay for this!' She got no further as the lion bounded towards her again. She screeched in fright and launched herself into the night air and away from the danger. This time she flew out of sight, all thoughts of revenge gone. She was simply glad to be alive.

Charlie and Singer hurried away to find the red caravan. Suddenly, they heard the noise of people approaching from all directions. Right in front of them Nasty Norman, the chimp's trainer, came running out of the darkness. Charlie turned around to find that Singer had disappeared and the white face of Happy Harry the clown was right behind him. Before he could flee, strong hands gripped the baggy shirt of his clown outfit.

'You're not one of our clowns,' snarled Harry. He lifted Charlie off the ground and stared into his face. Cold angry eyes seemed to penetrate into Charlie's head. 'You're a boy, an imposter. What are you up to?'

He dropped Charlie to the ground and gripped his arm so tightly that the boy cried out with the pain. 'Leave this kid to me,' he snarled at the circus folk who had all gathered round to find out what the commotion was about. 'I'll soon find out what he's up to.'

'He's wearing my shirt!' said one of the dwarf clowns.

'And my trousers!' said the other.

'Cheek!' they said together.

Striding rapidly away, the white faced clown dragged Charlie along behind. The boy stumbled and fell over several times, but Happy Harry pulled him back up to his feet and kept on going regardless. His caravan, black with a red stripe around it, was some distance away. Just as Charlie was pushed inside, he noticed it was parked right next door to a red caravan with several locks on its door.

Inside the black caravan, Charlie was startled to find himself face to face with a man he recognised all too well. It was Old Barking Mad or OBM for short. This was the name the children of Mercy Hall had called the former head of their orphanage. His real name was Jethro Barking, and he had been their most feared opponent in the past, but now, something about his appearance had changed. Although he still had a blotched, red face, he was much thinner and his eyes rolled and stared wildly around the room. His whole body twitched. Charlie drew back in alarm and tried to hide behind Happy Harry. But Old Barking Mad did not recognise his former pupil. In fact, he seemed barely to notice the boy's presence. His face had a vacant expression and he kept repeating everything he said.

'Give me the money, give me the money,' he gibbered, twitching his head from side to side as if trying to focus on the face of Happy Harry. 'Money I'm owed, so I am. Money I'm owed...'

Charlie had obviously interrupted a meeting between Harry and OBM and Harry was now keen to be rid of the crazy man and get on with sorting out this new problem. To his relief, Charlie found he was no longer afraid of OBM. Whatever he had been in the past, the man now before him was little more than a shadow of his former self. Happy Harry, he realised with a start, was an altogether different beast. This man was mean as dirt.

'You've got the creatures, you've got the creatures,' muttered OBM, scratching at the backs of his hands with dirty fingernails. 'Behind the hedge, behind the hedge. Freaks, freaks from behind the hedge. Now pay me, pay me. I want away from here, well away. Australia it is, Australia it is. Go now, must go now.'

Harry sighed in exasperation. Taking a wad of

money from his back pocket, he counted off several notes and handed them to the gibbering fool.

'You're as mad as a hatter,' he snarled. 'Take your money and go.' Opening the door he stepped aside and waved his visitor out. Having glared at the money for a moment, OBM twitched his head round, focused on the door, and lurched out into the night, stumbling and muttering as he went.

Harry slammed the door shut and smirked. 'Australia... Still not far enough...,' he said, more to himself than Charlie. 'Mind you, he brought me a fortune in freaks.' Realising he had said enough in front of a strange boy dressed as a clown, he stopped talking and turned his attention to Charlie.

'Why are you dressed like that, eh? What are you doing here? Looking for an audition?'

Charlie tried to tell the truth. 'We... I mean... *I* am trying to find a friend of mine. I think he's run away to join the circus, or somebody has taken him,' Charlie stammered and looked away. It sounded ridiculous to accuse the clown of taking Digby. What could a six year old boy do in a circus? Happy Harry obviously thought so as well because he laughed. It was a short grating laugh totally devoid of any humour. Then he grabbed Charlie by the shoulders and shook him so violently, Charlie felt his teeth rattle together.

The white faced clown stuck his head close to Charlie and hissed at him. 'I hate children! Nasty, noisy, always screaming and crying... Revolting little creatures, and YOU are no exception. Now tell me the truth or I'll lock you in the lion's cage. He'll soon make short work of you.'

Charlie stammered, but no words came out. He felt terrified and unable to speak.

'We?' snarled Harry. 'You said *we*. Who else is with you?'

Before Charlie could think of an answer, there was a loud knock on the door. Harry glowered at Charlie then reached out and swung the door open. There was nobody there. Holding Charlie by the arm he leaned out and stared all around the outside of the caravan. Nothing could be seen and nothing moved. Slamming the door shut, he pushed Charlie roughly against the wall. Immediately, there came a loud hammering on the door again. Harry was still standing by the door and he swung it open again. The clown was angry now and his hands reached out to seize whoever had the cheek to play games with him. But there was nothing to grab; the space outside the caravan was empty.

Oil lamps illuminated the circus in the early darkness of the evening. Harry peered into the gloom to see if anyone was near.

'Who's there?' roared the clown staring all around with a frown. He stepped outside and bent down to look under the caravan, but there was nobody there either. A puzzled look came over his face and again he looked around in bewilderment.

'Why don't you look up, you silly man? And why do you paint your face white? You're ugly enough without making it worse.'

Whirling round the clown looked up and, on the top of his caravan, a strange bird looked down at him. Was it a bird? Or was it a bat? He couldn't be sure. For a long moment the two of them looked at each other, then the creature, whatever it was, stretched out its bat-like wings and gave them a vigorous flapping. They made a clicking sound, rather like the ticking of a clock.

Harry had never seen anything like it in his life.

Batty flapped her wings again and leaned forward. 'What are you staring at?' she asked, then cackled in her usual taunting way. 'Have you never seen a talking Tick-Tock bird?'

Harry just stared in amazement. His jaw fell open, revealing two lines of crooked, stained teeth.

'You... What..?' he said, unable to finish even the simplest thought.

Batty launched herself off her perch and flew over Harry's head for a short way. Then, with a phoney squawk of pain, she fluttered to the ground as if she had trouble flying.

'A talking bird!' said Harry, snapping back to his senses. 'It's worth a fortune, if I can catch it! Come here little birdy,' he cooed and edged closer to the grounded bird. Then, remembering the boy inside his caravan, he hurried back and quickly bolted the caravan door. 'I'll deal with him later,' he muttered to himself. 'First, I need that bird...'

'Oh dear, I've hurt my wing,' cried Batty, as if in distress and she hopped a little way further from Harry. With a cunning look on his face, the clown crept towards the bird, making what he thought were comforting birdlike noises. As he edged closer to Batty, she fluttered and hopped a little further away.

'Oh, my poor wing, I might never fly again,' she muttered, making a good show of being in real pain. But out of the corner of her eye she watched the approaching clown and also looked beyond him at his caravan. When she saw the door open and close again she was satisfied that Singer had joined Charlie inside. It was time to move Happy Harry further away.

'Oh what's to become of me..?' she said, hopping further.

'I'll make you famous,' said Harry, following, his eyes flashing with greed.

Back inside Happy Harry's caravan, Singer and Charlie had found a set of keys.

'These must belong to the red caravan,' said Charlie. Slipping silently outside, they hurried over to it. After a glance behind them to ensure that the white faced clown was out of sight, they began to try the keys in the biggest lock. The first few did nothing, but the fourth key fitted perfectly.

'Got it,' hissed Charlie in triumph as he turned the key fully and released the lock. Soon all the locks were undone and Charlie opened the door.

Inside, there was an oil lamp on a table which illuminated the room. Charlie and Singer stepped inside cautiously. Simultaneously a gasp of astonishment escaped their lips. In a corner of the room two young girls with pale green skin and black bushy hair stared at them with large frightened eyes. Their arms and legs were tied together with rope so they could not move. One of them wore a yellow skirt and the other a red one.

Singer went to help them when a hiss came from the other corner of the room. Both of them gasped in surprise again. Also tied up was a young Snakehead. It was smaller than Charlie, with a yellow and black scaly body. Its legs were short and thick and its head was just like a snake. As the children stared at it in surprise, its tongue flickered out of a mouth full of sharp little teeth and its slit eyes stared back at them.

Immediately Charlie and Singer recognised the creatures as having come from behind the hedge. The two girls were Waterlanders from the lakes in the mountains. In a previous visit the children had lived in their village for a short while, and they knew at once the girl in the yellow skirt was Samsa. Singer rushed over and quickly untied their ropes. Immediately the two girls burst into tears of joy as they recognised Singer.

Charlie went over to the Snakehead. He had been a prisoner in the Snakehead village for a short time, and, though he pitied this one creature, he had no liking for Snakeheads in general.

'How did you get here?' asked Charlie in their strange, whispery Snakehead language. He knew them to be vicious, cruel creatures and was not keen on releasing even a small one, so he stood back and regarded it with suspicion.

'Men in orange robes caught me in the woods by my village. A big man put me in a sack. When I was let out, I was here with them two.' He nodded towards the Waterlander girls. 'I don't know where I am.' A tear slid out of the Snakehead's eye and Charlie began to feel a little bit sorry for him. He was only a youngster after all.

'Will you promise to behave yourself if I untie you?' he said in a severe voice. 'No eating people?'

'Oh yes, I just want to go home,' the Snakehead nodded its head vigorously.

'What's your name?'

'Lucius,' replied the creature as Charlie undid the ropes.

'What on earth are we going to do?' asked Singer, who was busy setting the girls free. 'We can't just leave them here, and there's no sign of Digby.'

'That clown was intending to use them as freaks in a sideshow,' said Charlie in horror. 'Old Barking Mad must have brought them through the hedge and sold them to Happy Harry.'

'I saw him leave the caravan earlier,' said Singer. 'He looked different somehow...'

'He's gone totally round the bend,' said Charlie. 'In Harry's caravan he kept gibbering something about Australia.'

'There is only one thing we can do,' said Singer decisively, 'and that is to get them all back to Mercy Hall as quickly as possible. Batty won't be able to

keep Happy Harry away for very long.'

'It's a long walk in the middle of the night; we can hardly take the train,' said Charlie in a worried voice.

'Come on Charlie! Bring that lamp and let's get going. The sooner we move the better. If Happy Harry catches us here we'll all be kept as freaks in a side show.' The panic in her voice was infectious, and as soon as Charlie translated for the benefit of the Waterlander girls and Lucius, all of them made a rush for the door.

Singer peeped out of the red caravan and saw a few people pass by and hurry towards a commotion happening on the other side of the caravan site. It seemed all the circus folk were there; she could hear a lot of noise and the occasional cheer. Whatever Batty was doing, it was working very well.

It was a strange procession that emerged from the caravan: two children, two green girls in coloured skirts and a snake-like creature. They hurried away from the caravans and cages and, after rounding the big tent, simply walked out through the main entrance and took the path they believed led to Erringford and the orphanage. There was no one to stop them, or even to notice them leaving. Batty had the whole troupe enthralled.

'Can't catch me for a bumble bee,' cackled Batty in delight.

She was perched on a flagpole at the far end of the circus field, looking down at Happy Harry, standing below and wringing his hands in frustration at his inability to catch the talking bird.

There was no secrecy now; a crowd of circus people had gathered round and were now also staring up at Batty with astonished expressions.

'A talking bird!' exclaimed Samson, the strong man. 'It's a miracle!'

'That is one valuable specimen,' said Dead Eye Dick, the human cannonball, though it wasn't actually Dick who went down the barrel of the cannon; he just lit the fuse at the back. 'If we could get our hands on that creature, people from all over the world would pay to come and see it. We'll make a fortune!' he cried, rubbing his hands together in delighted anticipation.

'I saw it first,' roared Happy Harry. 'It's mine.'

'Not if you can't catch it,' said Nasty Norman, who had visions of owning it himself.

'It will have to belong to everybody!' added Sir Montagu Twist, ringmaster and sole surviving half of the Brothers Twist, who had founded the circus together more than twenty years ago. Stepping through the crowd with an air of great authority, he

twirled his long, black moustache and looked up at the flapping bird appreciatively.

'It really is a fine specimen,' he said through clenched teeth.

'The bird's mine, I tell you,' cried Happy Harry desperately. 'It's mine!'

Nasty Norman had now come to the inescapable conclusion that Happy Harry knew more about the talking bird than he was letting on. He turned to face the clown with a deep scowl. 'Did that bird escape from the red caravan? We know you've got things locked up in there. What else are you hiding?'

A look of horror came over Harry's face. '*We*,' he cried. 'The boy said '*We*'! Somebody was helping him and I've left him unguarded! My treasures! He was after my little treasures!' He turned and started to run back to his caravan. The crowd followed him and Batty, realising that the game was up, flew away into the darkness.

5

BACK THROUGH THE HEDGE

The group decided to stop and take a brief rest by a post which had a bench seat next to it.

Charlie was leading the way with Samsa and her friend, Tarsa, close behind. The little Waterlander girls were used to an outdoor life; tough and wiry they had no trouble keeping up. Unfortunately the young Snakehead was not used to running. His little legs were short and, though he whizzed them back and forth as fast as he could, it was not quite quick enough. Singer was also a lot slower than Charlie and brought up the rear.

It was Singer who noticed the sign at the top of the post when she arrived, gasping for breath, to join the others on the bench. 'Look,' she said pointing upwards. There, at the top of the post, was a sign which said ERRINGFORD.

They all gave a sigh of relief. At least they were on the right road. The sign pointed to a path that they might not have noticed in the dark.

The lamp Charlie was carrying still burned brightly, but Singer was concerned its light may draw attention to them. 'Of course,' he cried in alarm, 'I should have turned it off ages ago; the moon is bright enough for us to see the path.'

'Quiet,' said Samsa suddenly, looking at Charlie. Charlie hushed the others. Her sharp ears had heard something in the distance and she looked intently back down the path they had just run along. Four shapes were emerging rapidly from the darkness making small grunting noises. Charlie felt panic rising in his stomach. They had been followed, and he had left the lamp burning, making it easier for the pursuers to keep them in sight. The shapes came so quickly that there was no time to hide.

'Hello, friend,' said Mo, his flat, brown face twisting into a gentle smile, as the four chimpanzees hobbled up and settled down beside them. 'We escape. Follow you.'

'You understand us. You friend,' said little Bee, moving closer to Charlie's side and taking hold of his hand.

Charlie looked down into her big brown eyes and realised that there was nothing he could do except take them back to Mercy Hall as well. 'All right,' he mumbled and sighed, 'but we must hurry. We have to keep going for a long time yet.'

'Far place?' asked Mo.

Charlie nodded.

'Good,' said Mo with a smile. 'Far good. Near bad.'

'Did anyone follow you?' Charlie asked Mo anxiously.

'No. All watching odd bird on pole.'

'Good old Batty,' said Charlie with a smile. 'We'd be lost without her.'

Charlie turned the lamp down as low as it would go, then started slowly along the path. The others followed. The moon lit up the way ahead. For a long time, they ran or walked in silence preferring to save their energy for the journey. In time, dawn broke and brought with it a pleasant summer morning, with clear skies and a sweet smelling breeze.

The group now found themselves straggling on the path alongside the large thorn hedge. Charlie recognised it and called out to Singer. 'It's the hedge! We're nearly home.'

A familiar tick-tock sound made Charlie and Singer look up. Batty was flying towards them, cackling cheerfully. They all stopped running and Charlie held his arm out to offer Batty a perch. But, as he knew she would, the bird plonked herself down on his head instead.

'Where did that lot come from?' asked Batty, glaring at the odd assortment of creatures gathered before her. 'Are we starting our own circus?' She dug her claws into Charlie's head, making him grimace.

'We are taking them to Mercy Hall. They have escaped from the circus and don't want to go back,' explained Singer.

'That's what you think,' Batty said, speaking quickly. 'Happy Harry and his friends have found out which way you went and are now close behind.'

'Then we must hurry. Come on everyone, we have to run again,' Charlie shouted in alarm.

'You won't make it to Mercy Hall,' said Batty, fluttering up into the air. 'They are riding horses and have dogs tracking you.'

'How long before they get here?' asked Singer, fear building up inside her and making her legs feel quite weak.

'Just a few minutes,' replied Batty. 'You have to hide.'

'Where?' asked Charlie looking around. 'There's nowhere suitable. We'll soon be caught.'

'Behind the hedge!' whispered Singer. 'If we can open it up and get through, the gap will close before Happy Harry gets here.' Immediately she gave out instructions. 'Batty, please find the square branch. It can't be too far away. There is a large sandstone rock right by it, now hurry!'

'Follow me,' Charlie instructed his exhausted companions.

Although tired, the thought of recapture gave them energy enough to keep moving at a steady pace along the path. A short while later, they saw Batty up ahead, flapping back and forth excitedly.

'She's found the stone,' gasped Charlie. He was well ahead of the others in the race to hide behind the hedge. He was also the only one strong enough to heave down on the square branch and he wanted the hedge to be open by the time the others reached it.

Singer looked behind her and saw a cloud of dust in the distance. 'Horsemen,' she thought, and looked anxiously to where Batty was squawking loudly ahead of them. She heard dogs barking and men cheering and realised they had been spotted by the pursuing riders.

When Charlie reached the sandstone rock, he spotted the square branch above it and leapt high in the air. Taking tight hold of it, he dangled for a moment until his weight slowly dragged the branch down. There followed a loud noise like the crackling of a million breaking twigs. Right in front of him a gap in the hedge opened up. All the branches within the dense hedge changed from growing sideways, twisted and tangled up, into thousands of slim, vertical poles that reached high up into the sky. The thorn gate was open.

Charlie knew the gate would only stay open for a few minutes. He needed to get everyone through safely before Happy Harry and the rest of the pursuers arrived. 'Come on, Samsa! Come on, Tarsa,' he yelled. The two Waterlander girls rushed passed him and dived between the long thin poles.

Lucius arrived next, his short legs moving in fast, jerky movements as he ran along with his snake head upright, his mouth open and gasping for breath. He crashed into the gap and forced his scaly body past the upright poles and joined the two girls on the other side.

Batty was flapping her wings frantically above Singer. 'Hurry, hurry,' she screeched. 'The dogs are nearly here.'

Singer was helping the four chimps to hurry along. Mo was carrying little Bee in his long arms as his daughter had just collapsed in the final effort to reach the gap in the hedge. 'Quickly, quickly,' howled Charlie, terrified the gap would close any second. He injected such panic into the chimps that they too just threw themselves in amongst the upright branches. The thick poles knocked them sideways and they bounced their way through, flattening the thinner ones in their panic to escape the barking dogs and screaming men behind them.

Singer shouted up to Batty. 'Stay this side of the hedge and go and tell the others what has happened.' Then, just as she stepped into the gap the crackling noise started again. The long slim poles rapidly bent in all directions, the branches twisted back to their original shape. Singer screamed in shock as the hedge started to crowd in on her. She darted forward but stumbled as she made the last few steps to safety. Mo stretched his arm into the hedge and, firmly grasping Singer's hand, he steadied her and pulled her through with a strong tug.

Charlie watched anxiously as the hedge closed. He saw the horses pulling up in front of the gap but the gate was growing thicker and it was too late for anyone else to squeeze past. He caught a glimpse of Happy Harry dismounting from his horse and the last thing he saw was the expression on Harry's face turn from smirking triumph to anger as the hedge snapped shut. He heard a lot of shouting and threats, but when the branches and leaves all finally came together, there was nothing but silence.

They knew that once the gap closed there could

be no contact with the other side until it was opened again. It seemed that the land behind the hedge existed in a strange invisible bubble that could only be entered when the hedge opened up. Nothing could fly over it and nothing could burrow under it. It was like a separate world, sealed off by a strange power, that none of them could fully comprehend.

Charlie kept the group huddled together by the part of the hedge they knew they could open. 'We just have to stay here,' he announced, translating for everyone. 'Happy Harry and his men can't get through the hedge, so all we have to do is wait. When they give up and go home, we can open the hedge and go back to the orphanage and decide what to do next.'

'We want to go home,' said Samsa, holding Tarsa's hand.

'So do I,' grumbled Lucius. 'I'm hungry.' He looked at the two little chimps and licked his lips.

Mo noticed the flickering tongue and stepped in front of his children with a stern look on his face.

'We stay with you,' said Flo, looking from Charlie to Singer. 'You friends.'

'We can't decide now,' said Charlie. 'We have to stay here and wait, but we must not move onto the grasslands.' He gestured to the wide fields that stretched out all around them and pointed a finger into the distance. 'Over that way is a land full of danger.' A frown came over his face and his eyes scanned the horizon in every direction. 'There are creatures here called Muttons that look like sheep, but they are not! They are vicious flesh eating animals that move slowly but live under the grass and can appear at any time. We must not wander off but stay where we are.'

Everyone agreed that Charlie was right and so the group huddled down to wait until the time was right for them to go back through the hedge.

It only took a few minutes for the circus folk to realise that the hedge was totally impenetrable. The thorns were thick, long and sharp. Samson gripped a thick branch and using his mighty strength heaved and strained to pull it out of the ground. A normal hedge would have been torn up by its roots, but not this one. Samson just went red in the face and had to give up. Some of the men tried to use knives to cut the branches but the wood appeared to be so hard the knives made no impression.

'Behind that hedge is a fortune for the circus,' said Sir Montagu Twist. 'We have to find a way through.'

Happy Harry agreed and gave instructions to one of his men. 'Willy, you take your horse and ride further on. There has to be a way through this hedge somewhere.'

'I know how to get through,' said Dead Eye Dick. 'I use gunpowder to fire the cannon. I have a sack of off the stuff back in my caravan. Enough to blow a hole in the hedge.'

Happy Harry laughed and clapped his hands

together. 'Yes, that will do it! Then, when we get our hands on those kids, we will make our fortunes.' A cunning look came over his face. 'And if there are more strange creatures and talking birds in there, we'll have them as well. Go on Dick be as quick as you can.'

6

BIG TROUBLE IN LITTLE AMBERWELL

Armed with a packed meal prepared by Mavis Minchcombe, Milly and Sam set out before dawn to visit Benny Smutt.

They used the carriage owned by the orphanage. It was a light two-seater carriage pulled by a single horse and it had become Scorpio's job to look after it and see to the welfare of the horse, Trotter. Scorpio was a young hunchback boy who had been born behind the hedge but had come back with George, Sam and Milly after their first trip beyond. Good with animals, he cared for Trotter, and had managed to turn him from a restless colt into a well-behaved and obedient creature. Although the carriage was designed for two people, Trotter was a big strong horse and could easily pull it along with a whole gang of children on board. Scorpio was also the driver and so went everywhere the carriage went. Dawn was just breaking when Scorpio called out 'Trot on,' and, with Sam and Milly settled in, the carriage rolled out of the stables and away down the drive.

It took two hours to get to Little Amberwell,

where Benny Smutt lived. It was a grimy town that had expanded around two factories; one an iron foundry and the other, a tannery, which kept the town busy turning animal skins into fine leathers. Unfortunately, the by-products of the tannery caused putrid smells to hang over the town and polluted the rivers, while the smoke and dust from the iron foundry made the buildings black and grimy. It was not a pleasant place to visit under any circumstances.

Trotter slowed down to a walk when the carriage reached the cobblestones at the edge of the town. A boy emerged from the doorway of a dingy terraced house wearing an oversized black jacket and a flat cap that pushed his ears out sideways.

'Stop here,' said Sam to Scorpio and called out to the boy. 'Do you know a chimney sweep called Benjamin Smutt?'

The boy barely looked up. He just waved his hand towards a chimney in the distance and said, 'Behind the foundry.'

It was easy to find. The foundry belched black smoke into the air which could be seen from anywhere in the town. By the time they reached it, people were crowding onto the streets, trudging to work, and horses and carriages of all shapes and sizes filled the muddy road, slowing the children down. The smell from the nearby tannery made Milly cover her face with her handkerchief.

'I don't want to stay in this town very long,' she gasped.

'You won't have to, look over there!' exclaimed Sam, pointing to a sign that read: Chimney Sweep.

Underneath was the barely legible name of Benjamin Smutt. The gate to the sweep's yard was open so Scorpio drove the carriage straight in and quickly turned it around in case a quick getaway was called for. Sam and Milly found a door which looked like it would lead to an office, but, in spite of knocking loudly for a long time, nobody answered.

'Is anybody looking?' asked Milly, as she took a long metal bar from the floor and prepared to lever the padlock away from door.

'No,' said Sam looking around carefully.

'Desperate measures are called for,' said Milly grimly and, with a great heave on the iron bar, she wrenched the lock from the door.

Inside a dirty and untidy room they found an old desk and several chairs. On the desk was a diary which had been left open at today's date. In the space, a single word – Mansion – was written.

'It could be that our sweep is working at a place called the Mansion,' said Milly flicking through the pages of the diary.

'That's just a name for a big house. It could be anywhere,' said Sam.

Slowly, they walked back to the carriage to find an old woman standing in the yard. She was dressed in a long black shawl and, being quite stooped, supported herself on a walking stick. When she peered at them they noticed she had a black patch over one eye.

'What are you doing here?' said the old crone in a rasping voice.

'Looking for Benjamin Smutt,' replied Milly staring at the woman. Then she added. 'Do you know a place called the Mansion?'

A cunning look came over the woman's face. 'I might do, but I don't like posh kids in a carriage.'

Sam pulled out a penny from his pocket and showed it to the woman. 'You can have this, if you tell us where Mr Smutt is today,' he said.

The coin was snatched out of his hand. 'If he's at the Mansion, it's a mile down the big toll road. Belongs to Lady Agnes Smithers, got huge iron gates. You can't miss them. Cleaning chimneys, that's what he'll be doing.'

Milly and Sam thanked the old woman and climbed into the carriage.

'Trot on,' called out the hunchback and in a few minutes they were on the road to the mansion.

The iron gates were open when they arrived so, with a tug of the reins, Scorpio swung Trotter past the stone columns and onto the gravel drive. A few minutes later, the mansion house itself came into view. It was a stately home of huge proportions, with more chimneys than it was possible to count, and was easily the biggest house they had ever seen.

'There must be a hundred rooms in there,' said Milly as she gazed at the house in amazement.

'If not more,' added Sam. 'So where do we start?'

Alongside the drive, as they approached the front

door, they could see gardeners working on huge lawns and beautifully coloured flower beds.

Scorpio brought the carriage to a halt alongside a large double door. A small flat roof provided shelter for guests arriving in inclement weather. The door itself was black in colour but fringed with a glistening, ornate yellow border.

'That door is covered in gold,' said Sam in awe.

'I don't care what it's covered in,' said Milly. 'All we want is Digby, then we can go home.'

By the time they dismounted from the carriage, the front door had opened and, filling the space behind, was a very large butler. He stood tall and straight and in order to look at the children without bending he had to peer down a large, purple-hued nose.

'What is it that you want?' he spoke with a very precise manner through tight lips that barely moved.

'We are looking for Benjamin Smutt, a chimney sweep,' said Milly most politely.

'I believe there is someone here of that name,' sniffed the butler, 'but as he is engaged in his duties, I'm afraid he is unable to receive callers, so go away.' The butler held both arms out and flapped his huge, red hands at them. 'Shoo, shoo, go away.'

Sam grabbed at Milly's arm. He could sense that she was getting angry and might do something foolish. Reluctantly she allowed Sam to escort her back to where Scorpio waited. 'I've got an idea,' he whispered in her ear.

Back in the carriage, he explained. 'Scorpio, just

go slowly and when that front door closes drive onto the lawn and take the carriage round to the back of the house in a big circle. We should not have gone to the front door - tradesmen go to the back of the house. A chimney sweep would never enter through the front door of a house like this.'

Scorpio drove Trotter rapidly round to the back of the house and there, parked on the drive, was a horse and cart that reminded them of Black Mike. It was black with soot and contained implements of the sweeper's trade with lots of empty sacks piled up in a corner. 'This time we don't knock,' said Sam.

The back door was open and they just walked in. A young maid was in a large kitchen peeling carrots. She looked up in surprise when the two children appeared.

'Where's the sweep?' demanded Milly.

'In the main dining room,' said the maid automatically.

'Kindly show us the way,' said Sam in his most superior tone.

'I don't think Mrs Simpson allows children in...'

'Now!' said Milly sharply and in a voice loud enough to show that she expected a prompt response.

The young maid dropped her peeling knife and, drying her hands on a blue apron, hurried out of the kitchen. The children followed.

The main dining room was down a long corridor. A large bony woman in a black dress and blue apron came out of the door as they arrived.

'Mrs Simpson...' stammered the maid.

Milly led the way. She brushed passed the housekeeper and entered the room. Sam was right behind her.

The housekeeper was not used to being ignored by children so she turned round quickly and grabbed at Sam's shoulder.

'Excuse me, young man!'

Sam turned and glared at the imperious woman.

'Madam,' he said in as firm a voice as he could muster. 'We are from the new Children's Inspectorate and we have reason to believe you are harbouring a stolen child in this building.

Taken aback, the housekeeper spluttered. 'Children's what?'

Inside the room, Milly marched straight to the fireplace where a small, fat man with a red face had watched their entrance in silence. He smirked as he saw the flustered housekeeper losing her otherwise stern composure, but his face changed when he saw the determination in Milly's eyes.

'Where's Digby?' she demanded.

'Don't know what you're talking about,' he sneered at Milly. 'Now go away before I take my strap to you.' He turned to the fireplace, crouched down and peered up the chimney. 'Go on, lad, get up there,' he shouted. In one hand he held the end of a pole, the other end was up the chimney and he pushed the pole hard up the chimney. There was a squeal from above. Milly and Sam recognised at once the voice of their friend.

'The lazy brat will clean that chimney or stay up there all day,' roared Benjamin Smutt, poking again with the long pole and eliciting another squeal from the poor lad.

Sam saw Milly clench her fists. Fearing the worst, he tried to persuade the sweep to allow Digby to come down. 'Please Mr Smutt, there's been a mistake. He's not an orphan.'

'And I'm no gentleman,' smiled Smutt. 'But there we are. It's a funny old world...'

'Let him come down or you'll be very sorry.' urged Sam, thinking perhaps it might be best to give him what-for after all.

The red faced little man turned his back on Milly and started to snigger, but his laugh was cut off abruptly as Milly placed her hands on his armpits and began to squeeze.

'Hey, what's going on?' he cried, as the small hands gripped him tightly. Then, with barely a sign of effort, Milly swept the sweep to one side and sent him sprawling across the floor and crashing into a large sofa.

'Don't get up,' Milly advised the startled man, who was rubbing at his sore head. 'Or I may be forced to throw you even further next time.'

Meanwhile, Sam was standing in the fireplace with his head up the chimney. 'You can come down now, Digby,' he called out. 'It's Sam and Milly! We've come to take you home!'

There was a scuffling noise from up the chimney and a small cloud of soot burst into the room. A rueful Sam emerged from the fireplace with his head and shoulders covered in black dust.

At that moment Lady Agnes Smithers bustled into the room, followed by her butler. She was a tall, angular woman with a face that seemed fixed in a permanent sneer. 'What is the meaning of this? I am taking coffee with Lady Prunella Aston-Poultney, and I am not pleased.' She spotted the sweep sitting on the floor, leaning in shock against the large sofa.

'Mr Smutt, may I inform you that *my* floors are not provided for *you* to take a siesta. If you wish to lay about all day, my man can show you to the stables! And who are these ghastly children?'

'They're from the Children's Inspectorate, Ma'am,' said Miss Simpson helpfully.

'The what?' cried her Ladyship. 'There's no such thing, and even if there were, I wouldn't have it in my house!'

No one knew quite what to say.

'Bentley,' said Lady Smithers turning to her butler. 'Have these people removed at once.'

'Yes, your Ladyship,' replied the butler, glowering at Sam and Milly.

'Honestly,' Lady Smithers continued as she bustled out of the room. 'I don't know what the world's coming to these days...'

As soon as she was gone, the butler turned to the children with a growl.

'I thought I told you...'

Just at that moment Digby jumped the last few feet to the ground and emerged from the chimney

in a cloud of soot. He staggered into the room with tears streaming down his face, his grubby hands wiping soot away from his cheeks. He was black all over apart from the whites of his eyes and, as he stood in the middle of the room, the only noise to be heard was the sound of his sobs.

'Mr Bentley,' said Sam in a reassuring tone. 'As I tried to explain, we only came to collect what is ours.' He gestured towards Digby.

'Well now that you have, see that you leave this place at once!'

Sam took Digby by the shoulder and headed for the door.

'Oi,' cried Smutt. 'That's my property!'

Turning his ire on the sweep, the butler snarled, 'As for you, Mr Smutt, kindly clean up this mess and take yourself away too. We shall not be needing your services any longer!'

As Milly, Sam and the recovered Digby headed for the main door, they could hear an argument brewing between the butler and the sweep.

'Best make it quick,' said Sam, hurrying Digby along.

'And on the way home, you can tell us what happened.'

Once they were all back in the cart, Scorpio gave Trotter an extra snap of the reins to get them back on the road home as fast as possible. Wiping the soot from his face with a rag, Digby told them his story.

'When we all went to the circus last Saturday, I met a clown who asked if I was from an orphanage. I said I was and he gave me a ticket for the evening performance and said if I came back on my own I could feed the animals. He said I wasn't to tell anyone because he only had one ticket to give away and all the others might get jealous if they found out he'd given it to me. So, instead of going to bed that night, I sneaked out of the house and went back to the circus. I know I shouldn't have done, but he gave me the ticket and...'

The boy began to weep. Milly put a reassuring hand on his shoulder.

'It's all right, Digby. Go on,' she said in a calm voice.

'I was told to find the clown with a white face called Happy Harry, but when I found him he put me straight into a closed carriage and took me to Black

Mike. Then I ended up with Mr Smutt. I thought I was a goner. It was awful!' Turning to look at Milly with moist eyes, he added, 'I'll never do anything like that again. I promise.'

It was early afternoon when they arrived back at Mercy Hall. All the children gathered around the carriage and cheered at the sight of Digby, with a big smile on his face. His mother, Mavis Minchcombe, hugged him so hard she almost smothered him with her apron, and all the time tears rolled down her cheeks.

'Thank goodness you're back.' said Robert to Sam and Milly. 'But I'm afraid Charlie and Singer are still trying to escape the circus people.' A worried look returned to his face. 'Batty came back to tell us they found two Waterlander girls, a young snakehead and four chimpanzees! Apparently they were all escaping from the circus and on their way here when the circus people chased them and now they are hiding behind the hedge.'

'How on earth did that happen?' asked Sam

'I'm uncertain of the details,' said Robert. 'Batty is keeping watch by the hedge and when the circus people get tired of trying to find a way through, we have to go and open the hedge so they can come home.'

They followed a happy Digby back to the house. He was telling his story to the children all over again, when the air was torn by the sound of an almighty explosion. Everyone stopped in their tracks and turned to see what had happened. A cloud of white smoke billowed in the air over the distant trees.

'It came from the hedge,' shouted Robert. 'What can have happened?'

'There's only one way to find out,' said Sam. Together, all the children turned and ran towards the smoke.

7

THE LANDS BEHIND THE HEDGE

Happy Harry stood with Nasty Norman and Sir Montagu Twist watching Dead Eye Dick light the fuse of his cannon. He had stuffed it with as much explosive as he could and it now stood pointing directly at the hedge.

'We'll blow it to smithereens,' smirked Happy Harry to the others. 'Then we'll find out what's on the other side.'

'Take cover!' shouted Dead Eye Dick as a small flame started chasing its way up the thin length of cord that led to the cannon's barrel. As the flame reached its destination, it went out. The circus folk hiding behind nearby trees held their breath. Moments later a loud explosion blasted from the cannon's mouth, sending a huge plume of dirty black smoke up into the air. When the smoke finally cleared, it revealed a giant hole in the hedge. Flames leaped in all directions, branches snapped and a smell of burning reached nearby nostrils.

'Wait for the flames to die down,' called out Harry. 'When the horses arrive, we'll go through.'

The men cheered loudly and gathered round the opening.

The explosion was heard on the other side of the hedge too.

The little group, who had been sitting quietly on the grass, leapt into the air with shock. The hedge shook violently and a hole appeared in front of them. Peering through it they could see a fire burning in the middle and they heard the cheering quite distinctly. Leaping to their feet the chimpanzees raced around in a panic and started to run across the grasslands. The two Waterlander girls rushed to stand by Singer and Charlie, while Lucius tried to bury his head in the grass.

'They've used a cannon to blow a hole in the hedge,' said Charlie in alarm. 'What do we do now?'

'We must run to Market Town and find Jangles,' said Singer quickly. 'If we can avoid the Robes, he will hide us, I'm sure.'

Charlie spotted the chimpanzees running wildly across the grasslands and called out to them. 'Come back here, Mo! Come back quickly!'

A few woolly sheep-like creatures appeared, seemingly from nowhere, near the chimps. 'Oh no,' cried Charlie. 'The Muttons are out.'

All over the grasslands the ground was stirring. Small lumps of earth grew bigger and bigger, then shaking off soil in all directions the Muttons emerged from their underground burrows. They didn't run. They moved slowly, attempting to surround any creature that strayed onto their land. Once surrounded, the flesh eating creatures would devour their prey in seconds.

When Mo and his family took a close look at the Muttons, they realised the peril they were in. The animals they thought were sheep had razor sharp triangular teeth set in wide, thin mouths. The Muttons approaching them were licking their lips in anticipation of the meal to come. Mo had no doubt what their fate would be. The chimps beat a hasty retreat back to the group.

Charlie explained what they were going to do. 'The circus people have blown a hole in the hedge, but they can't get through while the fire rages, which gives us a little time. We are going to find a friend who will help us. The last time we encountered the Muttons, we found that they love to listen to Singer singing. Stick close to her and hopefully we can walk safely past them.'

There were more Muttons than they had ever seen before. The noise and the vibration of the explosion seemed to have drawn every last one out onto the grasslands.

Singer started singing. She had a beautiful voice and the high notes stopped the Muttons in their tracks. A gap opened up in the crowd of dangerous animals and the small group was allowed to pass through safely. The Muttons nearest to Singer gathered behind, following the friends as they set off for Market Town.

By the time the fire burned out, Happy Harry and his men were ready to pass through the hedge. The children of Mercy Hall stood a little way down the path staring at the circus folk gathered around the hole in the hedge. There was nothing they could do, so they just stood and watched.

Happy Harry and Nasty Norman were the first to step gingerly past the dying embers of the smouldering twigs. The children heard Harry call back to his men. 'Come on, there's just a meadow here and a load of sheep.'

Sam smiled broadly and looked at Milly and Tod Beanpole, who was standing beside her. 'The Muttons,' he said. 'They've met the Muttons.'

'Do you think we should warn them?' said Tod, casually inspecting his fingernails.

No one replied.

A scream ripped through the air. It was not easy to tell if it was the scream of a clown in distress, or a ringmaster in distress, or indeed anyone else in distress, but whoever was screaming was, without a doubt, very afraid.

The men who had crowded through the gap in the hedge only a few moments earlier, now came streaming back out again, all of them with faces as white as Happy Harry. Harry himself was the last through the hedge. He came stumbling and gasping and clutching the seat of his trousers, which was torn, revealing bright red underwear that had obviously seen better days.

'Vicious sheep,' screamed Happy Harry. 'They've got teeth like sharks.' He turned around to see if the sheep had followed him through the hedge.

A dozen or so were gathered at the opening of the hedge and peering curiously at the strange new land on the other side.

'Shoot them!' screamed Happy Harry again, waving desperately at Dead Eye Dick, now standing a good way away.

'I haven't brought a gun,' said Dick. 'We're only chasing a bunch of kids!'

'Load the cannon!' screamed Harry.

Dick shrugged. 'I only bought enough for one shot. It's all gone.'

At that moment, a loud crackling noise made everyone jump. It came from the gap in the hedge. New branches were weaving their way out of the ground. Old branches bent by the explosion were straightening out and fresh, sharp thorns were popping into view.

The Muttons quickly retreated back through the hedge. As soon as they disappeared from view the hedge grew sideways and upwards, became tangled, leaves unfolded and, in a few minutes, silence reigned. The hole was gone, and the hedge stood as thick and impenetrable as before.

The circus folk stood and stared at the sudden and unexpected repair.

'It's unnatural,' growled Sir Montagu Twist. 'Or it's magic.'

'Oh no, it ain't,' snarled a very unhappy Happy Harry. 'Those kids opened the gap in the hedge and they must have done something on the other side to close it again. Let's look around. Maybe there is a handle or a switch of some sort.'

As the circus folk started to search for some other way to open the hedge, Robert gave a sigh of relief.

'We need to return to the Hall,' he said. 'The last thing we want is to be discovered by the circus folk.'

'What about the lever?' asked Tod. 'What if they find it?'

Robert shook his head. 'I don't think they will. It's hard enough for us to find, and they're just a bunch of clowns!'

So while the clowns continued their fruitless

search, the children headed home.

In the land behind the hedge, the bridge leading to Littlewich was crowded with Minlings looking curiously across the grasslands towards where the explosion had happened. They were small and skinny and wore brightly coloured shorts and tunics. Normally fairly good natured and content, there was a definite mood of anxiety in the air. Several small fingers began to point in the direction of the little group.

'There's no chance we can sneak through the town without being stopped,' grumbled Charlie as he spotted them. 'We've already attracted too much attention.'

'Can you see any Robes?' asked Singer looking anxious. She had stopped singing when the group came close to the bridge and the Muttons had returned to their grasslands.

'No.'

Although generally a passive people, the Minlings did not like strangers much, so when the odd party of travellers stepped onto the bridge, muttering voices began to rise.

'Peg them out!' one of the crowd shouted, and the others began to join in. 'Peg them out, peg them out.'

No attempt was made to stop the friends, but the children grew more nervous as they got closer. One of the Minlings, being bolder then the rest, stood in front of them to block their way.

'You must stay here until the Robes arrive,' he announced pompously.

Singer took a step towards him and, taking hold of the hem of her white dress, flapped it wildly at him. 'Shoo, shoo,' she shouted.

The Minling jumped in surprise. He wobbled backwards so fast that he fell and sat on his bottom with a startled look on his face. Those around him laughed and, taking advantage of the diversion, the children hurried over the bridge. Followed by a crowd of Minlings, they walked slowly along the river bank towards the warehouse where Jangles lived.

'We can't let this lot know that Jangles is our friend,' whispered Singer to Charlie.

'No, but how can we lose this crowd?'

'I think you should all stay here while I become invisible and go and see Jangles.'

Charlie agreed and the group stopped. It was difficult for Singer to become invisible without anyone noticing so she walked down to the water's edge and dived in. Just before she hit the water, she whispered 'Be invisible.'

The watching Minlings saw her disappear under the surface and waited for her to reappear. After a few minutes the onlookers started to mutter among themselves, then, they began to walk up and down the river bank looking for the missing girl. Charlie was the only one to notice the wet footprints that led out of the river and silently threaded their way through the crowd of Minlings and disappeared in the direction of the warehouse where Jangles lived.

It took about twenty minutes for Singer to return. She had borrowed Jangles' boat and had sailed in a long arc so that the boat appeared to arrive from the opposite bank.

'Oooh,' cried the Minlings when they recognised the girl driving the boat now speeding towards them.

Again the crowd watched with open mouths as Singer skidded the craft onto the bank. Quickly, Charlie ushered the chimpanzees, the snakehead and the Waterlander girls onto the boat, then he pushed it back into the water.

'Make way, make way!' called out a voice from behind the Minlings. Three men in orange robes pushed their way through the crowd. When they saw the boat and its occupants floating away from the bank, they screamed after them in rage.

'Interlopers! Apprehend them at once!'

One of the Robes waded out into the river and got near enough for Singer to see a man with a gaunt face stretched into a snarl. He was too late. Singer turned the engine to full power and steered the boat out into the middle of the river.

'That was a close shave,' said Jangles poking his head out of the little cabin at the front of the boat. 'I hope no one saw me.'

Charlie shook his hand warmly. 'So nice to see you again,' he said with a broad smile on his face. They had stayed with Jangles on their previous adventure behind the hedge, though nobody in Littlewich knew of their friendship. If the Robes found out, it would be the end of Jangles. The Robes pegged-out strangers, and anyone else who offended them, for the Muttons.

Staying well down in the bottom of the boat, Jangles told them that Jethro Barking, their former head of the orphanage, had been deposed as king of the Robes.

'He went mad,' he said, as the boat cruised close to the other bank. 'He wanted diamonds and precious stones from the NoGoodLands, but after one of his trips to that strange place, he came back completely doolally! I heard it said he deliberately went through the Rainbow Cave and stood at the front of the boat, instead of hiding in the cabin. None of the Robes who come from the Dome ever get changed, but the big king wasn't really a Robe He stood with his arms outstretched and screamed and laughed as lightning crackled round the boat.'

'That's why he went mad then,' said Charlie. 'He must have been changed in the Cave. I saw him at the circus and he was stark raving bonkers. Somehow, he found a way of opening the gate in the hedge and brought Lucius and the Waterlander girls with him.'

'The new leader of the Robes is called Bulkrit,' continued Jangles. 'He was the right hand man of the old king, but when the old king disappeared, Bulkrit conspired with OBM to make him king. Between them they became very rich, but when OBM went mad, Bulkrit took over and claimed he was to be ruler as there were no living descendants of the old royal family.'

'A lot has happened since we were last here,' said Charlie, 'but we haven't got time to worry about Old Barking Mad. Where are we going to hide until we can get back through the hedge? I don't want to stay here any longer then we have to.'

'Can we stay with you, Jangles?' asked Singer looking at him sweetly. 'We can sail about until dark and then land quietly at the warehouse,'

'Of course,' replied the Minling, but a worried frown crossed his face as he thought about the consequences of the Robes finding out that he had helped the strangers.

The two young chimpanzees were gazing out over the river and suddenly Bee tugged on Charlie's arm and pointed at three boats coming rapidly up behind them.

It didn't take Charlie long to realise who they were when he saw the orange gowns at the helm. 'The Robes!' he shouted in alarm. 'Quick Singer, head for the warehouse.'

Immediately, Singer turned the boat towards the quay in the distance. Behind it the warehouse loomed large. 'But we can't stay there,' she said. 'We'll soon be caught.'

'Then we'll have to go through the Rainbow Cave!' said Charlie in despair.

'Not with me on board,' said Jangles ducking back down into the cabin. 'Take my boat by all means, but as we pass the warehouse, I'll slip overboard and swim back. Oh, by the way, there's some bread and cheese and other things in a bag in the cabin.'

'Thank you Jangles,' said Charlie. 'We're so very grateful.'

Jangles smiles. 'It's been a pleasure... My days would be very dull without you lot turning up once in a while.' Then, with a look of sadness on his face, he asked, 'How's Batty?'

Charlie smiled. 'She's fine.'

'Oh good... Enjoying life over there, is she?'

Charlie nodded.

'I miss her, of course.' said Jangles. 'But there you go.'

'We're getting near to the warehouse,' Singer called, steering the boat closer to the quay.

Further up river, the water flowed slowly out of a tunnel in the side of the mountain. Any boat sailing through the tunnel had to go via the Rainbow Cave in the middle of the mountain. The strange power of the Rainbow Cave could make incredible changes in people. Milly had acquired her great strength there, Charlie had found he could speak any language, Sam discovered he could run fast and George was able to breathe under water.

'We have to go through the cave again,' said Charlie, addressing the rest of his crew. 'But it's dangerous. The changes are not always beneficial. People could easily lose the power of speech or sight as well as gain extra powers. Look what happened to Old Barking Mad! Everyone except Singer and I must stay in the cabin. We'll be safe because a person can only be changed once. You'll be safe if you don't see the rainbow.'

As they passed the warehouse, Jangles slipped quietly into the water and swam back towards the quay, unseen by the pursuers. Clutching at the wooden planks, he hauled himself up to watch the little boat, with the three larger boats close behind, disappear into the cave mouth.

'Bye everyone,' he said, quietly. 'Good luck.'

8

THE RAINBOW CAVE AND BEYOND

The complete blackness and quiet in the tunnel lasted a long time as they sailed slowly into the mountain. From time to time, the boat bumped into the walls on either side. As the air got colder, they huddled together to keep warm. It was a welcome relief when a faint light appeared in the distance.

As they sailed into the lake, a hazy mist settled the boat. A faint humming noise could be heard, distant at first, but growing louder as the white light increased in intensity. With the noise drumming in their ears, the white light suddenly changed, bathing the cave, the lake and the boat in a deep red.

'Keep inside the cabin,' ordered Charlie. 'It's starting!'

As the light pulsed through the spectrum, from red to yellow, green to blue, the atmosphere in the cave changed from a bright, sunny day to one dark and thunderous, scarred by searing flashes of forked lightning, sizzling and crackling all around them. Without warning, waves crashed against the sides of the boat, sending it rocking back and forth, like a child's toy in a tin bath.

Inside the cabin the Waterlander girls, the young snakehead and the family of chimpanzees put their hands over their ears, shut their eyes and tried not to scream. As the boat pitched and heaved, they were tossed around from side to side, banging arms, legs and heads against the wooden beams of the craft. The crashing of thunder overhead echoing their painful yelps.

The cabin doors flew open, crashing back and forth in a series of brittle snaps. Two pairs of hands flew up to seal them shut. Lightning flashed, eyes blinked, then met in the darkness, wide and shocked. They had reached a new level of understanding, of comprehension, of awareness, a shared new level that would leave them changed forever...

At last, as the colour of light finally changed to a soft violet, the thunder ceased, the waves receded and silence returned like a blanket to cover them in mute calm.

The boat sat in the middle of the lake, bobbing gently, as the last patches of violet mist drifted away into the darkness and the white light returned to brighten the scene.

'It's over,' Charlie whispered with breathless relief. 'You can come out now. We are nearly through to the other side.'

'Do we really need to go on?' asked Singer. 'There's a lot of danger on the other side of the mountain.' She shuddered as she remembered the Robes, the crocodiles, the sharks, the night-vultures and all the terrible and fearsome creatures they had met before. What new horrors might lie in wait for them this time?

'Or, perhaps you could take us home,' proposed Samsa, emerging from the cabin. 'We know this river goes through the mountain to the mighty waterfall that is the start of our homeland.' She looked beseechingly at Singer and added, 'I miss my family.'

'Samsa!' said Singer in surprise. 'You understood what I said without Charlie translating!'

'And she replied too,' added Charlie with a smile.

Singer looked deep into the girl's eyes. 'You've been changed. Did you come out of the cabin during the storm?'

The little girl looked embarrassed. 'When the waves hit the boat the doors burst open. Mo and I grabbed one each and shut them quickly. Mo had his arm round my shoulders when it happened and we both saw the blue lightning.' She looked at the chimpanzee as if to seek confirmation.

'She speaks truth,' said Mo, and when he realised he was speaking English too, his hand shot up to cover his mouth and his eyes opened wide with surprise.

'It looks like you've both got the same power as Charlie,' said Singer.

Samsa smiled happily at everyone, pleased with her new found gift, but Mo turned away, hunching his shoulders and scratching at his chest with nervous fingers.

'Did anyone else see the lightning?' asked Charlie looking at the rest of them and translating for the benefit of the snakehead and the chimps, but they had all stayed huddled in the bottom of the boat, their eyes tightly shut the whole time.

'How do you feel?' asked Charlie.

They looked at each other and one by one they said they felt fine.

'Well, we'll find out soon enough,' said Charlie grimly. 'I hope there are no bad changes.'

'There might not be any,' added Singer hopefully. 'Perhaps only Samsa and Mo were affected, and maybe they got the same power because Mo had his arm round Samsa.'

'Perhaps,' said Charlie with a shrug. 'Whatever happened, we need to keep going. If those other boats didn't follow us, then they'll be lying in wait for us, so we have no choice either way.'

Singer nodded in agreement and, swallowing her fears, took hold of the wheel once more.

The sunlight shone brightly as they emerged from the cave. As their eyes grew accustomed to the light, they saw a wide river in front of them, undulating through a pleasant green countryside. Anxiously they scanned all around for signs of danger. There was no sign of any Robes, although plenty crocodiles were floating about like discarded logs. None of them made any attempt to approach the boat.

'Keep to the middle of the river!' ordered Charlie. 'It's safer there.'

They sailed on, passing the Dome without

incident. It glowed and sparkled in the sunlight, but there was no one around and the place seemed eerily quiet.

'Keep going,' advised Charlie. 'We don't want to get stuck here. Not now.'

It was some time later that Lucius sat up in his seat and stared hard at the river bank. The countryside had changed to forest and the river become narrow and faster flowing.

'I recognise that old tree,' he shouted to Charlie in a high pitched voice. 'I've been there with the tribe.' They were floating up the middle of the river and Lucius was pointing to a great old tree whose branches stretched out over the water. Around the bottom of its trunk a large sandy area was clear of bushes and looked as if it had been well used by creatures drinking from the river. Everywhere else trees and undergrowth crowded down to the bank. It was hard to see any sort of break in the dense forest.

As they watched, two large Snakeheads came from behind the old tree and, shielding their eyes with their hands they stared out at the boat.

'Snakeheads,' roared Lucius again. 'Put me ashore!'

Charlie was only too glad to oblige. Having a hungry Snakehead on the boat was unnerving to say the least, even if he was only a small one. Singer guided the boat to the shore, and Charlie told Lucius to be ready to jump. He had no intention of exchanging pleasantries with a pair of full-grown Snakeheads.

Lucius stood at the front of the boat and called out to the two Snakeheads standing on the little patch of beach. They waved in response and stared curiously at the approaching boat.

Charlie leaned over the side and looked anxiously at the water to see how deep it was. Raising his arm, he motioned to Lucius. 'I can see the bottom of the river, it's shallow enough for you to jump.' Then he called to Singer. 'Turn the boat or we'll run aground.'

Frightened of the water, the young Snakehead missed his chance. Singer spun the wheel and the boat responded by swerving violently to one side, making Lucius teeter on the edge. Desperate not to get wet, the young Snakehead managed to step away from the edge, but fell back into the bottom of the boat. With a deep thud, he landed on the two baby chimpanzees, who squealed with surprise as they wriggled out from under the scaly body of the squirming creature. Bo grunted and grabbed hold of Lucius' feet. Bee, seeing what her brother was doing, grabbed hold of the Snakeheads' hands. In perfect unison, they lifted the young fellow up and threw him over the side.

Lucius roared, hissed and spluttered as he flew through the air and splashed into the water, only yards away from the small sandy bank, and sank beneath the surface. Moments later, when his feet found solid ground, he stood up still gurgling and

hissing.

'Good bye, Lucius,' Charlie waved. He couldn't help but laugh at the sight of the dripping wet creature being dragged out of the river by his two companions. 'Good luck!' Singer turned up the engine and the boat roared back out into the middle of the stream, safely away from the bank.

Daylight faded and night came slowly as the boat sailed up river. It was never completely dark in the land behind the hedge; there being always a faint glow in the sky as if the sun had been switched off and a night-light turned on to replace it. The bag of food and water left by Jangles was shared out to the starving crew. Charlie took over steering the boat, allowing Singer to eat and get some rest.

The two Waterlander girls had grown very fond of Bee and Bo and slept in a big huddle in the corner of the little cabin with their arms around the little chimpanzees. The chimp's parents, however, stayed awake - ever watchful, ever wary. This was a new land to them, full of strange sights. Anything might happen.

Just after dawn, the noise of a large waterfall brought them all to the front of the boat. When they sailed around a bend in the river, they saw the towering cliffs that surrounded the lake. Right in front of them, the waterfall that signalled the end of their journey cascaded down the mountainside. The land of the Waterlanders lay on a high plateau that could only be reached by a difficult mountain path or a secret passageway that led up from a cave behind the waterfall.

'Over there!' called out Samsa pointing to the side of the waterfall where the forest stopped and the high cliffs began. 'The cave we want is over there.'

Nervously, Singer sailed to the side of the lake. She felt safe in the boat and was well aware of the dangers that lurked in the forest. In addition to the Robes and the Snakeheads, she had heard unknown creatures calling to each other in the night; the memories of their calls came back to haunt her, sending a shiver down her spine. As the boat approached the shore, she imagined hidden eyes lurking in the undergrowth, watching their arrival.

The boat banged against the river bank, the water

beneath slopping with a thick, muddy sound. As if in answer, there came a low rumbling, grunting noise from a plant standing near the water's edge. It had small yellow fruits hanging from branches covered in large pointed thorns. Though there was no wind, not even a gentle breeze, the bush swayed gently from side to side.

Singer yelped in fright.

'Don't worry,' Charlie whispered to reassure her. 'It's a Polly Tree. I'll talk to it.'

He had met Polly Trees before. The bush was actually a living creature with a head deep inside the branches, and roots that could be pulled up out of the ground if they had to move. But this was not something they were keen to do, preferring instead to stay in one place if they found it to their liking. It was a Polly Tree that had saved their lives once before by opening up its branches to reveal a snug area inside the bush where they were able to hide from danger.

'I see you,' Charlie spoke in the language of the Polly Trees, a rumbling and grunting sound reminiscent of distant thunder. 'I am a friend.'

'Welcome, two legs. I have heard of you. You must be careful. In this forest are many dangers.'

'Such as?' asked Charlie.

'Many feet come and go. Angry feet with cruel intent; but today is quiet. You can walk safely in the forest. We shall warn you if we hear the feet of others.'

Once the boat was tied up safely by the Polly

Tree, Charlie spoke to it again. 'Have you seen any Waterlanders lately?'

'Waterlanders? These two are the first I have seen in many a moon.' The Polly Tree waved a thorny branch at the two Waterlander girls as they climbed out of the boat. It then turned its attention to the family of chimps, jumping and cackling on the bench.

'You have new creatures with you. What sort are they?'

Charlie was about to reply, but it was Mo who spoke up in the Polly tree language. 'We are Chimpanzees, if you please! Good day to you!'

Charlie laughed. Mo was beginning to enjoy his new found skill.

'I would touch you,' said the Polly Tree, and immediately a long thin branch waved out over the group and settled on Mo's shoulder. The rest of his family screeched with alarm. Bee and Bo jumped back into the boat. Flo tried to drag Mo away from the tree.

'Don't worry,' said Mo to his wife. 'It's only a tree being friendly.'

The Polly Tree stopped swaying and the thin branch was withdrawn quickly. 'I hear a noise in the sky!' it said with a new urgency. 'It is a sound I have heard before.' Everyone stopped and listened, staying as quiet as they could. Sure enough they heard a humming, whizzing noise, somewhere up in the sky, and coming straight towards them.

'It's Tod Beanpole!' shouted Singer excitedly as

she looked up and saw the rocket boy flying straight over the lake and heading for the top of the waterfall.

'There are three of them,' laughed Charlie with delight as two other figures with rocket rucksacks appeared over the trees, following Tod towards the top of the high cliffs.

Singer shielded her eyes as she tried to identify the two others. 'I think the little one is Milly, and I'll bet the other one is Sam.' She felt a wave of relief spread over her as she watched them disappear over the cliffs. The special powers of Sam and Milly always made her feel a lot safer when they were around. 'WE'RE HERE!' she shouted and waved towards the top of the cliff.

'They can't hear you,' grunted Mo. He was right, the cliffs were very high and the noise of the waterfall drowned out any sound.

They could see the top of the cliffs through the leaves and overhanging branches of the forest. A tiny figure appeared at the top and looked down at them. Singer and Charlie waved like mad.

The figure stood motionless looking all around the forest but it didn't wave back. 'They can't see us,' said Singer in despair. 'The trees are in the way.'

'Let's see if the trees can help us,' said Charlie and he turned to the Polly Tree. 'You're bigger than we are. Can you wave your branches? Our friends at the top of the cliff can't see us?'

'Glad to be of assistance,' rumbled the tree.

They jumped back in surprise when the Polly Tree waved all its branches, shaking violently from top to bottom. It then added to this display a roar like a clap of thunder. Charlie, Samsa and Mo understood the roar. 'All who can hear, wave your branches!'

Milly and Sam joined Tod at the top of the cliff. 'Can you see anything?' asked Milly.

'No,' he replied gloomily. 'They could be anywhere in the forest, or already up here where the Waterlanders live.'

'Look!' said Sam pointing at the trees. 'Some of the trees down there are being blown about like wild, but there's no wind.'

'They're just bushes,' said Milly, staring hard at the roof of the forest below them. 'Maybe some animals are rooting about and making them shake a bit.'

'They weren't shaking a moment ago, now they're all doing it; blowing in a wind that doesn't exist,' said Tod excitedly. 'And what's more, they're Polly Trees!'

'If they're Polly Trees,' said Milly, 'they are not being blown in the wind, they're waving to us. Charlie and Singer must be with them.'

'But where exactly are they? There are loads of Polly Trees waving. Which one is sheltering Singer and Charlie?'

All together they waved back from the top of the cliff.

Peering up through the branches Singer saw them wave. 'They've seen all the Polly Trees,' she cried.

Charlie told the Polly Tree it could stop waving,

but instead the tree gave out another huge roar that made the friends jump back again it was so loud. 'Stop waving,' it cried, and in an instant all the swaying branches were still.

Above them Milly, Tod and Sam watched as all the Polly Trees stopped waving. That is, all except the one by the river bank.

'That's where they are!' exclaimed Tod. 'And I can see the back end of a boat sticking out from under the trees.

Again they all waved, but this time directly at the one tree still waving.

'They've seen us,' said Singer with excitement.

'You can stop waving now,' said Charlie to the Polly Tree. 'And thank you so much for helping us.'

'Here comes Tod,' exclaimed Singer.

'Scatter,' shouted Charlie to the chimpanzees and the Waterlander girls. He knew Tod crash-landed almost every time he used his rocket rucksack, and now he was coming straight at them.

As Tod approached the ground, he misjudged the distance as usual and crashed into the trees above the children, bouncing wildly off their branches, before landing right on top of the poor Polly Tree itself.

'Grurk!' roared the tree, as Tod disappeared inside its branches.

There was silence for a few moments as the friends gathered round the tree, peering into the thorny depths.

'Where am I?' came a plaintive cry from within.

There was a rustling noise as the Polly Tree reset its leaves and branches.

'Yikes,' came a frightened shout from Tod, 'there's a big head in here and it's looking straight at me. Help!'

'Be quiet,' ordered Charlie. Then he spoke to the tree. 'Can you please let our friend out? He didn't mean to hurt you.'

'I am not hurt, just a little surprised to meet him so suddenly.'

Slowly the branches of the Polly Tree opened to reveal a crouched and worried looking Tod Beanpole staring out at them. 'Hello,' he said. 'I'm so glad we found you.'

9

THE DOWNWARD SLOPE

The sudden and unexpected reunion lifted their spirits and gave them fresh hope. They swapped stories about their different adventures, especially how the Waterlander girls and the chimps had been rescued from the circus, and also how Digby had been found once again, albeit up a different chimney.

Everyone agreed that, as they were now together, they should escort Samsa and Tarsa back to their village. Charlie was troubled by the Polly Tree's news that no Waterlanders had been seen for a long time, and wanted to be sure they got home safely.

The walk to the Waterlander village was long and tiring, but everyone kept each other's spirits up with hopeful talk and the odd cheerful song. But when they got near to their destination, silence fell and the cheer evaporated.

The village came into view, but there was no sign of life and no noise at all. Normally children would be swimming in the lake or running around shouting, but all was ominously quiet.

The village was built in a clearing on the bank of the lake. When the little party came out of the trees and saw the village just in front of them, Samsa and Tarsa went running on ahead. The others walked slowly towards the thatched huts, fearing the worst.

The village was deserted. When the others joined Samsa and Tarsa in their family home, the little Waterlander girls were crying. They searched every hut, but it was clear that all the Waterlanders had left, taking most of their belongings with them.

'Where is everybody?' sobbed Samsa. 'Have the Robes taken them?' Banging her fists on the sandy soil, she cried, 'They always wanted more of everything! The diamonds from the hills and the pearls from the bottom of the lake. They wanted us to be slaves, work for them day and night.' A ghastly thought struck her, and her eyes widened at the horror of it. 'That's it! They must have taken my people to the Dome to work as slaves!'

'Let's search the forest,' said Charlie putting his arm round Samsa. 'If they left in a hurry we might find a trail.'

Samsa nodded and gave him a little smile.

At their feet, Mo began to jump up and down, beckoning to Flo.

'We search. Good at finding trail.' Looking at the Waterlander girls, he added, 'You look after little ones. They look after you.'

Leaving Bee and Bo behind with the Waterlander girls, the two adult chimpanzees ran out of the hut and off into the forest, sniffing and scratching at the ground as they went.

Small amounts of food were found in some of the huts, so they had a meagre meal together. Charlie suggested they prepare provisions for the journey back. 'If the Robes have taken all the Waterlanders, we have to rescue them.'

'Impossible,' said Sam shaking his head. 'Even with our powers there are far too many of them.'

'And they are big and violent,' added Singer sadly.

Tod was standing in the doorway of the hut and looking out over the lake, constantly scanning the area for any signs of an enemy. His eye had caught sight of something glistening on the lake. Staring intently into the distance, he soon realised what it was.

'There are boats on the lake and they're coming this way,' he shouted to the others, who rushed out to join him and see what they could see.

'Maybe it's all the Waterlanders coming back?' said Singer hopefully.

'There are a lot of boats out there,' murmured Sam as they stood in a line on the sand, hearts beating with hope.

'They look like Waterlander boats,' said Samsa, a tremor of excitement in her voice.

'I'll go and see,' said Tod, strapping on his rocket rucksack. With a quick flick of the lever, he rose into the air. A mere second later, he came straight down again, landing with a thump and falling into a crumpled heap. 'It's the Robes!' he spluttered, through a mouthful of sand. 'I can see orange gowns in every boat. There's no sign of the Waterlanders.'

Samsa let out a desperate cry.

At that moment Mo and Flo came running out of

the forest, both gasping for breath.

'We found trail and followed. Passed Polly Tree. Spoke with it.' Mo paused for breath, pleased with himself for having been able to talk to a Polly Tree.

'What did it say?' asked Samsa impatiently.

'Many Waterlanders pass, about a week ago. They carry bags and bundles. Women and children cry.'

'Where were they going?' asked Samsa in anguish.

Mo shrugged. 'Polly Tree said hide in the hills. After them come Robes with weapons.'

A heavy silence fell upon the group.

'Robes return next day,' said Mo, continuing his report in heavy tones. 'But not Waterlanders. They don't come back.'

Samsa was thinking. Charlie had a sense she knew something the rest of them didn't. The two Waterlander girls whispered together in low urgent voices before Samsa spoke. 'They must have gone to the Forbidden Cave. It's up in the hills... somewhere.'

'What's the Forbidden Cave?' asked Milly, a little puzzled. And why would they go there if it's forbidden?'

'It doesn't matter!' said Tod, his eye still on the approaching boats. 'We have no time to spare. The Robes are coming. If the Waterlanders are in the cave, then that's where we have to go, and quickly.'

Tod was right. The children scrambled to grab their rocket rucksacks, their belongings and as many provisions as they could carry.

Once they were ready, Mo and the chimpanzee family scampered ahead of the children to lead the way. Their swinging gait looked ungainly, almost comical, but covered the ground quickly. The path led past the Polly Tree but they didn't stop, though Charlie felt obliged to thank the tree for its help. 'Thank you, Polly Tree, we are in your debt. Perhaps when we return we can chat some more...' He rumbled the few words as they followed Mo and clambered up the hill.

The trail narrowed and turned into a steep mountain path. They all trudged slowly along in single file, keeping safely away from the edge.

The entrance to the cave was not hard to find. The ground leading to it was trampled down and it looked as if a lot of people had been there very recently. Mo was very worried about the approaching Robes, so he climbed a tree and looked down at the lake.

'I see village,' he called down to the children, who stood in a group looking at the low, dark entrance to the cave. 'Robes arrive and search.'

Milly turned to Samsa and her friend. 'What do you know about this cave? Is it safe to go in? Are your people hiding in there?' she asked.

'I don't know. It's supposed to lead to the Valley of Secrets,' said Samsa nervously. 'It's called the Forbidden Cave because if people go in there they don't come out again. No Waterlander ever goes in.'

'Maybe there are miles of narrow caves and passageways and everyone gets lost if they explore,' said Charlie peering into the heavy darkness of the cave's interior. Even Milly, the smallest of them would have to bend down to squeeze in through the entrance.

'Someone has to go in,' said Sam. 'I'll do it!'

Nobody argued with him.

Inside the cave, Sam was met by complete darkness. He placed one foot carefully in front of the other and moved very slowly forward, his heart pounding with fear. Gradually though, with each step, the cave grew brighter and he began to see the ground in front of him. Breathing a sigh of relief, he made better progress.

Turning a corner, he came into the main cavern and found it fully lit up. He looked around to find the source of the light and saw a glowing ball high in the roof of the cave. At the far end of the cave was another opening, almost square, set in the floor and guarded by a rail with posts that were hammered into the ground. One side of the cave was flat and strange writings had been carved into the wall.

'Are you all right?' An anxious voice he recognised as belonging to Singer floated into the cave.

Realising his friends outside were nervous and anxious for him to return, he made his way out.

'It's amazing,' he said to the rest of them as they pulled him out of the entrance. 'There's no danger in there, apart from a hole in the ground. I saw a bright light in the roof and rails around the hole. There's also writing on a wall, but I can't read it.'

'And what about my people?' asked Samsa, urgently.

Sam shook his head. 'There is no sign of any Waterlanders.'

Milly was bursting with curiosity. 'Come on then, let's all go in.'

'Mo, will you keep an eye out for Robes?' Charlie called up to the chimpanzee who was still at the top the tree. 'I'd hate them to arrive and trap us in there.'

Mo nodded and gave a short wave.

Flo and the little chimps wanted to stay near Mo, so they also remained behind. Sam led the way and the children entered the narrow passage. Moments later they were staring around in wonder at the brightly lit cavern.

'That light, it's amazing,' said Charlie. 'It's not an oil lamp, so how does it work?'

'I don't know,' said Tod. 'But it's like some I've seen in the Dome. Some very clever people put it there. It must be a light that burns forever.'

'I wonder where that hole in the floor goes?' said Singer. 'It's angled into the mountain and it looks very steep. It's like a giant slide.'

'It must go to the Valley of Secrets,' said Samsa quietly.

'Or it could just go to the centre of the earth and sudden death,' said Tod gulping and staring wide-eyed at the hole in the ground.

Milly was staring at the writing on the wall. 'Samsa, if that was written by the Waterlanders, maybe you can read what it says?'

'Waterlanders don't read or write,' she said, looking at the strange writing and shaking her head.

'Charlie, you can speak in every language. Can you read the writing?' asked Milly, suddenly remembering Charlie's power.

Dragging himself away from the hole in the ground and the light in the roof, Charlie walked over to the wall and stared at the unfamiliar, scratched out letters. His brow furrowed with concentration. 'I believe I can,' he said.

For a while he muttered to himself then slowly he read it out loud: *The Search for Knowledge is a One Way Journey.*

'What can that mean?' asked Singer.

'Wait a minute. There's another line underneath,' said Charlie. Concentrating hard, he read it out slowly. *For Thinkers the Only Way is Forward.*

'Our ancestors used to be called Thinkers,' said Samsa. 'Maybe they wrote the strange words? Perhaps they could read and write in those days?'

'Perhaps,' said Sam thoughtfully. 'The one way journey could be referring to whatever is at the bottom of the hole. Maybe we'll find the answers to the magic light, the mysteries of the Dome, and find out who wrote on this wall.'

All eyes turned to the hole in the ground. 'It's a long way down,' said Milly, then added slowly, 'With no return!'

'Only because the slope is too steep and slippy to scramble back up,' said Singer. 'Perhaps if someone wearing a rocket rucksack went down, then, if there was nothing down there, they could simply shoot themselves back up again.'

'That could be difficult and dangerous,' said Milly. 'Especially if it goes round bends. Which of us would be daft enough to try that?'

They all turned to look at Tod.

'No,' he said, gulping and backing away. 'I don't like holes in the ground.'

Nobody else wanted to volunteer so they shuffled their feet in the dust and tried to think of another idea.

'I could fly over the mountain,' suggested Tod looking pleased with his idea. 'If there is a valley on the other side, I can look for the bottom of the tunnel and when I find it I'll come back and tell you all about it.'

'We don't have time for a long search,' said Milly, folding her arms. 'The Robes are coming...'

Tod's face fell. 'Oh,' he said, 'I hadn't thought of that.'

Singer was examining the floor of the cave. 'A lot of people have been here. Look at all the scuff marks. And what's that over there?' she wondered, staring into the far corner of the cave.

Samsa was nearest to where she was pointing. She darted into the corner and picked up a small shoe. 'It's a Waterlander shoe. It must belong to one of the children.'

'Then they have been here!' said Charlie emphatically. 'And with the Robes right behind them they were probably chased down the hole in the floor.

Tod leaned over the hole. 'Halloo,' he shouted down the hole. 'Is anyone down there?'

Everyone stopped talking and strained their ears, but no reply came.

A moment later there was a clamour from the entrance to the cave. The chimpanzees were jabbering all at once and calling out to them. They rushed out in alarm. Mo was descending from the tree and the little chimpanzees were bouncing up and down, shouting.

'Robes nearly here!' cried Mo racing towards them and gathering Bee and Bo up in his arms. 'Must go somewhere!'

'Well,' said Milly. 'We have no choice now. We have to stick together, so we may as well all go down the hole.'

'Please Milly,' said Mo. 'We'll be safe in the trees. We don't want to go into the cave. The Robes will never find us in the forest.' He was frightened and anxious to escape. 'We'll stay close to the Waterlander village and wait for you to return.'

They had grown fond of the chimpanzees and were reluctant to leave them. But Mo was adamant, and certain he could look after his family whatever trouble came, so the children hugged them quickly and said goodbye. Then the chimpanzees ran to climb the nearest tree and the children headed back into the cave.

Tod had already strapped on his rucksack and said quietly, 'I'll go first. If everything is all right down there, I'll shout back up to you. If you don't hear me shout, think of something else...' Without saying any more, he stood up straight, took a deep breath and marched to the edge of the hole. Sitting down, with his feet dangling over the edge, he closed his eyes and pushed himself onto the slide.

For a few moments they heard him swishing down into the mountain, then all went quiet. Behind them a noise made them turn around. The first of the

Robes had arrived in the cave. His orange hood was down and wild eyes glared at them with triumph. The sleeves on his gown were rolled up and in his pale hands he carried a heavy stick.

Samsa and Tarsa screamed in unison and jumped into the hole together.

Milly didn't hesitate. She turned to face the Robe with a gleam in her eyes and a grim smile on her face. The Robe made the mistake of ignoring the small girl and went to attack the two boys standing by the hole. As the Robe rushed passed her, Milly swung a skinny arm and her clenched fist hit the big man in the stomach. It was a punch of enormous power and they all heard the breath rush out of the stricken man's mouth. He dropped the stick, stopped in his tracks and doubled over with pain.

'There'll be more of them here in a moment,' said Milly calmly. 'We'd better go.'

Sam looked at her with admiration. 'I wish I could do that,' he said as he threw the two remaining rucksacks and a bag of provisions into the hole. Then he sat down on the edge of the hole and, closing his eyes, pushed off.

Singer and Milly looked at each other for a moment. 'Good luck,' said Milly.

Singer nodded grimly and slid into the hole. Milly looked around the cave, almost wishing more Robes would arrive. A fight would be preferable to leaping into a black hole.

'Go on,' said Charlie 'You first. I'll be right behind you.'

Taking a deep breath, Milly sat on the edge and followed the others.

Just as Charlie sat down, two more Robes appeared, clubs at the ready. Charlie looked at them and smiled.

'So long, fellas!' he cried, and was gone.

10

THE VALLEY OF SECRETS

The noise of the screaming girls filled the tunnel. It was the only sound Milly could hear as she whizzed at high speed down the slope.

The slide was long, fast and bumpy. Milly was forced to lie on her back, the rocket rucksack clutched to her chest, her head bouncing against the smooth stone beneath her. She was starting to feel quite dizzy when the frantic pace began to slow. Gliding gently round a corner, she saw the light of an opening ahead. The ground beneath her changed to a sandy soil and she slid gently out into a brightly lit valley.

Standing in front of her and looking out over the valley were Singer, Sam, Tod and the Waterlander girls. Scrambling to her feet and feeling relieved to be alive, Milly joined them. Right behind her was Charlie, who landed with a joyous scream.

'That was amazing!' he cried, jumping to his feet. But the scene that greeted his eyes, made him stop and stare like the others. The exit from the tunnel was situated on a low, sandy ledge with the floor of the valley stretched out in front of them.

It was a scene of utter chaos.

A battle was raging under their very noses. Down

below the ledge and lined up behind a ragged stone wall were the Waterlanders. The green-skinned men were standing in tight rows, wielding long, heavy sticks and lunging and swiping at small, squat black-legged creatures that swarmed around the other side of the wall. Behind the men, a group of women and children were gathering rocks and stones and rushing them over to the men who hurled them at the enemy.

The friends stood and stared in amazement. The two Waterlander girls were the first to move. They jumped from the ledge, rushed towards the women and immediately started to help.

'What *is* that?' said Sam, as a black legged creature took a leap from the top of the wall, pushed by the others coming up behind it. It looked a little like a giant spider, but with only four short, black legs and prominent staring eyes in the front of its shell like body. It was so big, it came up to the knees of the Waterlanders. On its back, a thin tentacle protruded and lashed from side to side. As they watched, one swipe from the waving tentacle knocked a Waterlander sideways and he fell to the ground, as if in a daze.

The creature's big eyes stared about, cleverly assessing its surroundings. With a swish of its long tentacle, it brushed past the Waterlander men and headed straight for the women and children. The gap it created was closed as Waterlander warriors moved sideways, lashing out with their heavy sticks as more of the horrible creatures clambered over

the wall. Two of the men tried to stop the creature, but the swinging tentacle kept them beyond striking distance.

The Waterlanders were obviously in desperate trouble. As the black-legged creature swatted a Waterlander child with its lash, Milly gave out a shrill cry of rage and leaped from the ledge to help. There was a pile of heavy sticks just below them. Charlie, Sam and Tod followed Milly in the race to join the battle, each grabbing a stick on the way.

The women and children were scattering as the spider-like thing spread fear and havoc amongst them. But then, an angry Milly arrived with her fists clenched and her arms waving. The black-legged creature was taken by surprise as a whirlwind of heavy punches landed on its back and brought it swiftly down.

Milly realised that the tentacle on the black scaly back was a weapon. As it swung back to lash out at her, she reached forward and grabbed the slender tendril with a strong left arm. A pungent smell came from the top of the stalk, making her feel quite faint.

'It must have a poisonous tip,' she thought. She reached out her other hand and, quick as she could, tied the stalk into a knot. Jumping back, she grabbed the creature by its forelegs, raised it up and hurled it back across the wall. It landed in a confused heap, right in the middle of several of its comrades, taking them all down with it.

With a sense of victory building inside her, Milly turned her attention to the defenders lined up on the wall. A heavy stick lay on the ground near a fallen Waterlander warrior. She picked it up and, in a few strides, was standing on the top of the wall between two startled Waterlander men.

'Come on!' she cried, 'Tally-Ho!' and set about the creatures with a fearsome ferocity that gave those around her renewed courage.

Whack! Bang! Wallop! The blows rained down thick and fast. Milly cracked the back of every spider that came within reach. Soon a gap appeared in front of her as the enemy learned to keep out of her way. As she edged sideways to help the defenders, she heard a familiar whooshing noise. Looking up she saw that Tod had taken to the air to join the fight. He was hovering just above the monstrous hoard, waving his heavy stick back and forth.

Down below, everyone momentarily stopped fighting to watch a sight they had never seen before; a rocket boy in action. Curiosity soon changed to panic among the attackers, as they all collided in their efforts to get out of his way.

In fact, Tod had lost control of his rocket. It was whizzing around like a balloon, dragging him to the left, then to the right, then and up and down at high speed, whilst the boy underneath it squealed and shouted with fright. At one point, the rocket scraped Tod along the ground. He tried to run with it to keep his balance, but that didn't work and he found himself dragged at speed into a mass of retreating vermin. Skidding along the ground, he scattered the black creatures left and right until finally they turned and ran in every direction just to avoid him. He roared again in fright as the rocket shot up into the air and came down again, bouncing him up and down a few more times, before he finally managed to yank the lever into the stop position.

As he ground to a halt, dazed and confused, a small smile spread across his battered face. The fight was over. The black-legged creatures were running down the slope and away into the distance.

Behind him, there was silence. He turned to face the stunned defenders with a huge, embarrassed grin on his face.

'That was fun,' he said, and the Waterlanders erupted into a great cheer and jumped over the wall to crowd round their new-found, if unwitting, hero.

A great celebration followed.

Samsa and Tarsa were reunited with their families, all flooding tears of joy. At the same time the Waterlander warriors carried Tod and Milly shoulder high round and round the makeshift huts that constituted the Waterlanders' new village. The people were so excited and pleased they would have danced all day, if they hadn't been so exhausted from fighting. Very soon, tiredness set in and the shouting and cheering settled down to quiet conversation and fresh preparations.

'Come,' said Bredon, placing a hand on Charlie and Sam's shoulders. 'We have much to discuss...'

The friends found themselves ushered into a large, solid hut which had become a meeting place for the whole tribe. They were already acquainted with Bredon, the leader of the Waterlanders, and a man they called Red Headband, the father of Samsa and a brave warrior. However, there were more Waterlanders in this new village, and the friends became aware that although they all had the same green-hued skin, there was amongst them a separate group who were slightly different. For a start, they were smaller in stature, but with larger heads and wider eyes. In all they seemed to be much more fragile looking than the Waterlanders from the top of the slope. It was a wonder to the children who they might be and where they came from.

Charlie was sitting next to Bredon, preparing to act as interpreter for the discussions, when a group of very old Waterlanders entered the hut in a solemn procession and made their way to a raised platform at the far end.

'Who are these lot?' asked Charlie, in a low whisper. 'And what's going on here? What happened to your old village?'

'Once again we are in your debt,' replied Bredon. 'Dear friends, your arrival was most unexpected but very welcome. You are indeed formidable warriors.' Then, in a hushed and respectful voice, he leaned close to Charlie and explained.

'These others are kinsmen of ours, descended from our own ancestors.' He gestured towards the small procession and added, 'They are the elders of their village.'

He sat back, expecting the elders to address the room. But they were slow, taking their time to settle, so he leaned towards Charlie again. 'We have lived in adjacent valleys for many generations with no contact at all. They are called Thinkers. But, they tell us, at one time we all lived together in the Dome. We were so pleased to find them when we arrived here a few weeks ago, fleeing from the Robes...' He was silent for a while, chewing over the memory with gritted teeth. Then he grabbed Charlie's arm and carried on. 'But they too are beset by an awful enemy - the Scarrogs!'

Charlie swallowed, his throat dry. 'You mean

those spider-like things we fought off?'

Bredon smiled and patted Charlie on his knee. 'When all seemed lost, you and your friends arrived. I cannot thank you enough.'

'Did you all slide down into the valley like we did?' asked Charlie.

Bredon's smile faded and he looked down. 'Yes. It was a terrible decision we had to make, but when the Robes attacked us in great numbers, we had to save our families, and our lives, so we hid in the cave. One of our bravest men volunteered to explore the hole in the ground. When he called back that we should follow him, so we did. And here we are.'

At the front of the room the elders had finally settled themselves on large, patterned cushions. One of them, his head a tangled mass of wispy, white hair, framing a sad, lined face. His deep blue eyes scanned the room carefully, moving slowly from face to face. He wore a long, yellow tunic draped over his thin shoulders which reached all the way down to bony ankles, on the end of which were a pair of surprisingly large feet.

'That's Merfan, their most venerable leader and a very clever old man,' whispered Bredon.

As Merfan raised both arms, the room became silent.

The old man spoke in a quiet yet commanding voice. 'The people of the Waterlands are united again. Today's victory over the Scarrogs shows us there is a chance for us to survive. Our new friends from the distant world, of which we know nothing, have proven their courage and their friendship. For this we thank them from the bottom of our hearts.'

He put his gnarled hands together, placed them over his heart, then gave a little bow of the head towards Charlie, Singer, Sam, Milly and Tod. Following his lead, everyone else in the hut did the same thing. An appreciative mumble hummed around the room, until it was stopped by the elder raising his hands once more.

'And now, our brave new friends will provide us with the knowledge to drive the Scarrogs into their swamp and keep them there for ever!' His voice rose as he spoke, and his eyes gleamed with a sudden, ferocious energy. 'Our search for the knowledge of our ancestors will soon be over!' His eyes blazed at the children, and all other eyes locked on them too. The air fizzed with breathless expectation.

Charlie squirmed in his seat. He felt enormously embarrassed, having no idea what on earth the man was talking about. Milly, Tod, Sam and Singer looked at him expectantly, waiting for him to translate for them. He did so, and they all stared back at Merfan with bewildered looks on their faces. None of them felt they held any knowledge that could be of use to the Waterlanders. Charlie was about to speak, when the old man made another announcement.

'We have no time to waste,' continued Merfan. 'Back to your posts! Your elders must speak with our saviours before the Scarrogs attack again.' He smiled happily at Charlie.

There was a lot of clapping and shuffling of feet

as the room emptied and most of the Waterlanders left.

When the children and the elders were alone, Charlie asked hesitantly, 'So how do you think we can help, exactly?'

Merfan leaned forward and spoke quietly. 'Our ancestors settled in this valley so long ago, we know nothing about them or where they came from,' he said with a shrug of his bony shoulders.

The other three elders gathered around him, nodding in agreement. 'Legend tells us that after we settled here, a mighty shaking of the earth threw up the swamp and split the valley in two. Our ancestors, who lived where the swamp is now, all perished!'

Merfan nodded vigorously. The other three heads shook.

'The only thing that remains of their ever being here at all is that building you can see up on the cliff. We believe that building contains the history and secrets of our race.'

Merfan took a deep breath and continued. 'For many generations, we have never been able to leave this valley. But it supplies us with all our needs, so why should we? The land is fertile and we grow all our food. For centuries, we had no enemies and no need of weapons. That is, until the Scarrogs emerged from the swamp...'

Now all heads shook in a sad unison.

'At first there was no problem. They were small things, we could tread on them. But then, gradually, and I mean *ever so* gradually, they grew bigger and bigger. And suddenly, for no reason we could understand, they attacked our village, without warning!'

'Perhaps you trod on too many,' said Charlie, with a grin.

Merfan continued, ignoring the remark. 'Without proper weapons, we were vulnerable, but we beat them off with heavy sticks. This happened time and time again. We learned to fight them but, as I have told you, the Scarrogs were getting bigger. We were so relieved when our cousins walked out of the cave and spoke our language. They have been teaching us to fight in better ways, and have helped defend us from the most recent attacks.' He nodded towards Bredon, sitting at the back of the tent on a big cushion.

'We were only too pleased to help,' said Bredon. 'We couldn't fight the Robes in our own land, but we had to help you. We have nowhere else to go,' he added practically.

'Why couldn't you find out the secrets in your building?' Charlie's curiosity was aroused and, after he had translated all the old man said, the other children also had lots of question to ask.

'The building was partly buried in rubble during the mighty shaking of the earth. For generations our people worked and scraped the rock with whatever tools we could fashion. Finally, we uncovered the entrance. Inside, we found strange lights inside, and machines that hummed and a voice that spoke from within the walls...'

'It must have been an exciting moment,' said Charlie.

The old Waterlander shook his head sadly and gave a short shrug.

'Nobody could understand what it said. Over many generations our language had changed too much, or our ancestors spoke differently to us.'

'There are many different languages in our world,' offered Charlie. 'That is why my gift is so useful.'

The old man smiled. 'That building is now on the other side of the swamp and we can no longer visit it. When I discovered you had this gift to understand any language, I knew you would be able to understand the voice from within the walls and discover the lost secrets.'

The old man smiled, and tears of joy welled up in his eyes.

'Our destiny is within reach,' he croaked, and the three other heads smiled and nodded in vigorous agreement.

'Excellent!' said Charlie. 'So how do we get there?'

'Ah,' said the old man, raising a thin, bony finger. 'That's the tricky bit!'

II

ACROSS THE SWAMP

'Or perhaps not..' said Merfan, thinking again. 'That machine you have... Can it fly far?'

'I'll say!' said Tod. 'As long as you can stop to recharge from time to time.'

The Old man's eyes lit up. 'Then perhaps there is a way.'

Early the following morning a crowd gathered on the defensive wall to watch the attempt to reach the building. In front of them, the ground rolled downwards to the swamp. Already the Scarrogs had emerged from the water and were scuttling back and forth, tearing at the ground in what looked like a very agitated state.

'There seem to be more of them every day,' exclaimed Merfan, 'and I'm sure they are still getting bigger.'

Alongside him another ageing Thinker nodded in agreement adding, with a worried frown, 'Something has changed in the swamp over recent years. It looks the same, but something is affecting the Scarrogs. Look how quickly they move and how aggressive they are. It was never like this before.'

'Where's Tod?' asked Charlie, looking around. He

and Milly were both strapped into their rucksacks ready for the flight. It had been arranged that once they were safely over, Tod would join them, but first, he was going to create a diversion.

'I'm here,' they heard Tod shout, and he staggered in front of them carrying four sticks with bundles of rags tied to each end. He climbed onto the wall and announced that as a major part of his diversion, he intended to frighten the Scarrogs with fireballs. 'Light them up,' he called out to Bredon, who promptly put a blazing brand to the end of each stick. Both hands now full of rapidly burning fire sticks, Tod found he couldn't reach his lever.

A frown crossed his face as he realised his predicament. Turning to Singer, who was standing next to him, he said, 'Turn the lever, old girl, and watch me go.'

Cautiously, Singer reached out and did as he asked. Tod took off with a whoosh. The rocket took him in a searing arc towards the swamp, the sticks burning fiercely in the wind. With flames leaping out behind him, he looked like a shooting star as he sped across the land and over the scuttling Scarrogs. It was a performance that certainly attracted attention. A great mass of Scarrogs followed the rocket boy as fast as they could.

'Go,' shouted Charlie, once the Scarrogs were out of the way. Flicking their levers, he and Milly set off together, making straight for the building half way up the rock face on the other side of the swamp.

'Can the Scarrogs reach the building?' asked

Sam, observing the steep ramp running from it down to ground level.

'Oh yes,' replied Merfan grimly. 'But as long as they don't see your friends enter, they'd have no reason to. Hence the diversion.'

They looked across the swamp, to where Tod was flying wildly back and forth, leaving twisting trails of smoke in the air behind him.

'Do you think it's working?' asked Singer.

'Look at them,' replied the old man, pointing his bony finger at the scuttling black creatures running in circles, in vain pursuit of the crazy flying boy. 'It's working.'

Landing on a narrow ledge in front of the door, Charlie and Milly clutched at the jutting rocks to hold themselves tight. The door was high in the rock face. The ramp below led straight down to the swamp. It was steep and covered in slimy green algae.

'Do you think the Scarrogs can climb that?' asked Milly, peering down.

Unsettled by the height, Charlie peeked quickly over the edge.

'No way,' he said, uncertainly. 'Too steep.'

'So how do we open the door?' Milly asked, keen to get off the narrow ledge as soon as possible.

Charlie examined the smooth, metal panel in front of him.

'I don't know,' he shrugged. 'They got it open before, so maybe we just...'

Before he could even say the word, his hands pushed against the door and it slid open with a barely audible hiss. Startled by its sudden opening, Charlie stumbled into the room behind, only just keeping his balance. Milly followed, unstrapping her rucksack as she went.

Leaning both their rucksacks against the wall, Charlie and Milly gazed in wonder at their new surroundings.

They were in a small room, about ten feet square and the same in height; a perfect cube. The walls of the room were white, but shone with an ethereal, unreal glow. They could see quite clearly, even after the door slid shut of its own accord, cutting out all daylight.

For a moment there was complete silence, then a voice filled the room. Whirling round Milly and Charlie tried to locate its source, but it seemed to come from everywhere and nowhere at the same time. It was a man's voice, speaking in an insistent monotone devoid of emotion. However, the Thinker had been correct in assuming Charlie would understand the words being said.

'Do you know what he's saying?' Milly asked.

'Yes, but you'll have to be quiet. He's giving instructions.'

Milly waited quietly as Charlie listened carefully, mouthing every word. When the voice stopped, Charlie walked to the wall opposite the door and stared at it. There were no markings on the wall, but Charlie reached up as high as he could placing the palm of his hand on the surface as though he knew exactly where to put it. Then, he traced an imaginary circle as wide as his arm would let him. That done, he stepped back to stand by Milly.

'Well,' she asked, fizzing with excitement. 'What did he say?'

'He welcomed us and said that valuable information is contained in this building,' Charlie replied in a quiet voice. 'Then he said to share in the secrets of his people, I should draw a circle on the wall.'

Both of them stared in mute surprise as a picture appeared where Charlie had drawn the circle. A round screen on the wall showed an image of an old man with green skin and a large head covered in white hair. Wearing a white tunic with short sleeves, the man was obviously a Thinker.

The man started speaking again and Charlie listened. Milly, desperate to know what was being said, had to bite her lip to keep from interrupting. Suddenly, Charlie held his hand up high, palm facing out. As though responding to his command, the voice stopped and the picture on the wall froze with the speaker's mouth half open.

Charlie turned to Milly, a smile stretched across his face.

'The man is from the past,' he explained. 'A long, long time ago. He speaks differently to the Waterlanders, and the Thinkers, but he also said we could listen to anything in this Building of Knowledge, because every language is available.'

Milly frowned. 'I don't understand.'

Charlie tried to explain. 'It's almost like the building itself learns from you. All a person has to do is to talk to the wall for five minutes, on any subject, and the man will talk back in the same language. If I want him to stop talking, all I have to do is to raise my hand. And I raise it again to make him continue. It's fantastic.'

Charlie chuckled at the wonder of it all.

Milly shook her head in unbelieving amazement.

'Go on,' said Charlie. 'Talk to it.'

She hesitated, then strode boldly up to the wall and started talking to the frozen image of the Waterlander. She told it about how they discovered the hedge, and of their first journey behind it, and how the children now ran the orphanage... In fact, she got so carried away, Charlie had to step in to make her stop.

'He doesn't want your life history. He just wants your language.'

With Milly silent, Charlie raised his hand. Immediately the Waterlander resumed talking, only this time it was in English. It sounded a little odd, rather like a man imitating Milly's voice. Milly stood dumbstruck.

'You may ask me questions,' the Waterlander said. 'But remember, I have been dead for many, many years and I may not have the answers. In fact, nobody will ever hear my messages if this building crumbles into the mountain, as I fear it will.' For a moment, a sad frown crossed the old man's face.

'Where did you come from?' asked Milly.

For a moment, the man, or the machine behind the man, was quiet, as though thinking about the question. But then, it spoke.

'From a place outside this planet, further from the moon, further from the sun. From another world far off in a distant galaxy.'

'From the stars?' said Milly breathlessly. 'Incredible!'

'How did you get here?' asked Charlie.

'Our ship crashed on this planet many generations before my birth. Some of my people wanted to stay, but others wanted to repair our vessel and seek another planet which was more suitable.' A sad look came into the man's eyes as he explained. 'At first we battled with the creatures who already lived here.

Men, like us, but giants, twice our size, but only very primitive, with a very low level of intelligence.'

'How did you survive?'

'Many perished before we harnessed the power of our ship to create the barrier that kept out the giants.'

'Charlie,' interrupted Milly. 'I can hear something, outside...'

Charlie listened. There was a noise, a clattering and a squeaking, a scratching at the door.

'Scarrogs,' he said at last. 'They must have climbed up the ramp.'

'We need to get out of here and back to the others.' said Milly anxiously. 'Ask about weapons.'

'Did you have weapons?' asked Charlie, crossing his fingers and hoping that the old Waterlander could help them in their predicament.

'We were a peaceful race,' said the man, 'intending only to discover, not to conquer. We had but one weapon of defence.'

'We really do need that weapon right now,' said Charlie.

'Where are the weapons?' asked Milly impatiently.

'All our knowledge is stored in the rooms behind me. There is a door next to this screen. It is audio locked, but you, who have shown intelligence comparable with my people, may enter. Just call out the name of our home planet, Zendora.'

Charlie stood back and called out loudly, 'Zendora.'

The room seemed to come to life, the lights brightened and a huge door next to the screen slid open. A humming noise from the room inside seemed urgent and busy; the children half expected workers to be bustling about their business. But when they looked inside, there was no one to be seen, though what they did see, startled them. It was more than just a room, it was a huge warehouse, going back as far as they could see, with long corridors separating row upon row of packing cases stacked high to the ceiling.

'This building goes back into the mountain,' said Milly in astonishment. 'The bit at the front that we can see from the Waterlanders' wall is just a gateway to this place. What on earth is in all those cases?' She tilted her head back, staring at the endless rows.

'Maybe this will help,' said Charlie. Directly in front of them was a pedestal with a screen attached. Instinctively they both approached the pedestal and climbed three short steps to find a thick book lying on top of it.

'Everywhere's so clean and bright but according to that old Waterlander man nobody has been here for centuries,' marvelled Milly.

Tentatively Charlie stretched out a hand and opened the book. It didn't look old, though it must have been ancient, yet the pages were thin and without creases or stains. They both looked at the first page. The words on it were written in a strange language. Just as Charlie furrowed his brow, trying to see if he could make sense of them, they all slowly changed shape. The lines were all squiggly to Milly, but as she watched, the written words moved around and she realised they were changing into English.

'Oh my goodness,' she breathed. 'This is magic.' She turned to look all around in case some strange creature from another world was close by, causing all this to happen. But they were alone, and their presence was bringing on the change.

'Look,' said Charlie, 'it's like an index to a book.'

At the top of the page they read - *History*. Then under that, the word - *Zendora*, followed by a whole lot of numbers. The next word was - *Beginning*.

'Is that proper ink?' said Charlie, staring at the page. Reaching out a finger, he poked at the word. Instantly the screen in front of them burst into life with a picture, then a voice started talking as well.

Milly screamed with surprise and fell backwards off the pedestal. Crouching on the floor she stared up at the screen, flickering with images of walking, talking people. It was strange, and very unnerving.

Charlie seemed able to cope with it and understood better what was going on. 'It's science and technology way ahead of anything in our world,' he said excitedly. 'It is a book, but the information is in pictures, with people talking. We've just gone to the chapter that explains how the Waterlanders and the Thinkers got here. Let's watch it.'

'No' said Milly. 'This is all very interesting, but it's making me feel nervous. We need to get back to the others. We can come back for a history lesson later. Find something that will help us.'

Reluctantly, Charlie agreed and scanned down the pages. 'What about this?' he said, pointing to a heading which read: *Jetpack Instructions*. 'We've got two of those with us.'

'We know about those!' snapped Milly. 'Find some guns or something useful!

But Charlie had already touched the words and before Milly stopped speaking, a picture of the rocket rucksack burst onto the screen. In front of Charlie, the page of the book had also changed and he read:

'To use as a Flying machine.

To use as an energy source.

To use as a weapon.

To use as a light.'

Milly was soon leaning over the book with him. 'There!' she said triumphantly. 'The jetpacks are weapons as well. If only we'd known!' And she poked her finger on the word *weapon*.

A Waterlander man appeared on the screen wearing an identical rucksack to the ones they had with them. The man stared out from the screen, smiled and then started talking. 'Swing the jetpack from the back to the front,' he said. Expertly, the Waterlander demonstrated by sliding the strap off one arm and swung the pack round so that it was over his chest and both shoulders carried its weight.

'Take hold of the flight exhaust tube, and twist it upwards. Then push.' As they watched, he extended the tube. It narrowed as it lengthened until it stretched out in front of him and looked more like a gun. 'It is essential,' he continued, 'that only the minimal damage is caused to any enemy creature that needs to be immobilised.'

The Waterlander took hold of the starting lever adding, 'Pull the lever out and the ray gun is in stun mode. It will emit a yellow ray that will render unconscious any creature it makes contact with. The range is about one hundred paces. The effect is temporary, of course, but how long it lasts depends on the size of the creature.'

The face smiling at them from the screen took on a solemn expression. 'In extreme circumstances, the lever can be pushed further towards the jetpack. The red ray then emitted is lethal. I implore you to be most careful in arriving at the decision to use it.'

Turning sideways, the man raised the gun to take aim and fired a slim red beam at a nearby target. It was a brief burst of energy that shot out of the extended tube, but the impact on the target was devastating. The whole thing burst into flame and shattered in seconds, leaving little more than a pile of smouldering ash.

'It is important to use the rays only in short bursts, as each firing uses a great deal of energy. After prolonged use, the pack will need to be recharged.'

Finished with his demonstration, the Waterlander smiled and made a slight bow, at which point the screen went blank.

'Well I never,' said Milly, shaking her head. 'We've had a deadly weapon all this time, but we never knew it.'

'Probably just as well,' replied Charlie. 'We might well have killed somebody without meaning to. Especially *Tod*! He's a danger to life and limb just flying. What would he be like with a ray gun?'

'A frightening thought,' agreed Milly.

The scratching at the main door had grown louder and more frenzied.

'But for now, I think we've got some Scarrogs to deal with.'

Charlie frowned. 'Shouldn't we maybe practise first?'

'Yes,' agreed Milly. A loud scrape at the door made them both jump. Black claws began to prize the doors open.

'But I don't think we have time!'

12

BATTLING SCARROGS

An overpowering smell of stagnant swamp, accompanied by a ferocious buzzing sound, made Charlie and Milly take a step backwards. They only just had time to strap on their jetpacks before the door was ripped open and the Scarrogs began to flood in, like a swarm of angry bees.

Charlie twisted the lever on his pack and the yellow beam shot out, stopping the nearest Scarrog in its tracks. With a few sideways steps, its legs gave way and the stunned creature sank to the floor. Another Scarrog took its place, looking straight at Charlie with small, unblinking eyes. In a flash, the lash on its back snapped back, then whipped forward. It was so quick, Charlie only just managed to fire another burst of the yellow beam before a slug of thick, gooey liquid splattered on his chest.

Three things happened at once. The first Scarrog recovered and clambered back to its feet. The second sank down as if taking a rest. A third jumped onto the back of the second and whipped its lash towards Charlie.

Milly was ready, her pack set to red: Kill!

Her beam hit the third Scarrog right between the eyes. It shot backwards out of the doorway, tumbling back down the steep slope, taking a few of its comrades with it.

Shifting the beam to the first Scarrog, now fully recovered, she gave it a full blast on the side. There was a brief, high pitched scream before its shell disintegrated. The second Scarrog, recovering from the initial stun, had also got to its feet. Milly gave it a short, well-aimed blast and sent it careering backwards down the slope.

Milly now had the range. As soon as another Scarrog appeared in the doorway, she blasted it out of sight with the deadly red beam. Five or six times she cleared the doorway before the Scarrogs realised that further attacks would not work. As the attackers retreated, Milly moved to the doorway and looked out. The Scarrogs had retreated back down the slope to form a large semi-circle of buzzing, angry creatures.

Milly smiled. 'That showed them. They'll think twice before coming back!'

She expected to see Charlie by her side. Instead, he had dropped his gun and was walking round the room in circles with a look of complete bewilderment on his face.

'Charlie?'

He gave no answer but for an indistinct mumble.

Milly heaved the door shut and rushed over to him. 'Are you all right?' she asked, terrified in case he had taken a direct hit from a deadly lash.

'It's the smell,' he said, his eyes wandering about the room. 'It's horrid and I feel all weak and dizzy.

I need to sit down.' He dropped to the floor and slumped against the wall, his uncoordinated hands trying in vain to wipe the gunk from his shirt.

'Does it hurt?' asked Milly, kneeling over him.

'Not really... Just stinks. Very odd.'

'The lash must be used to disable their prey and help them to catch whatever living thing they want.'

'Merfan said they eat anything,' said Charlie, remembering something the Thinker had said. He blinked a few times and seemed to be returning to his old self.

'They've gone,' Milly assured him. 'At least for now...'

It was a good ten minutes before Charlie felt his strength returning. When he felt able, he took up his jetpack, strapped it over his chest and pushed the lever in. 'No more messing around with the yellow ray where the Scarrogs are concerned,' he said, a look of determination hardening his face. 'Let's go and teach them a lesson?'

Milly smiled with relief. When Charlie collapsed she had feared the worst. His recovery gave her renewed hope.

'Stand back,' he ordered and threw the door open.

This time, none of the Scarrogs charged at it. Instead, they stood in the same semicircle buzzing and moving about restlessly, but always keeping a cautious distance.

Milly shut the door behind them and they started the journey back to the stone wall. Edging along, back to back, with their ray guns set to red, they inched their way down the slope. The going was steep and slippery. They had to be careful not to lose their footing completely. An escort of Scarrogs followed them, keeping pace with their every step, and after a few metres they realised they were surrounded by the creatures.

At first, there was no attempt to attack. Then, with an extra loud, angry buzz, one of the largest of their number broke out of the seething crowd and raced towards them. Milly raised her gun and fired the red beam directly at it. The light bounced in front of it at first, but Milly kept the lever twisted until she saw the beam sweep across the front of the Scarrog's face. Once hit, the Scarrog fell over its front legs and collapsed in a crumpled heap on the ground.

They continued to edge their way along, the circle of clattering vermin moving with them like a fixed ring of menace. The nearer they got to safety, the more agitated the Scarrogs became. A lot of them scurried around the ring, buzzing angrily. One of them made a dart at Charlie and he fired a red beam at it. He missed with the first shot and the red beam shot into the crowd of Scarrogs behind it. His second beam stopped the attacker in its tracks.

Time and again, separate Scarrogs charged at them. Each time they picked off the individuals with no problem, but they realised that if all of them charged at once, they wouldn't stand a chance. The fear was, the Scarrogs might realise this too. There would be no surviving if the enemy got organised.

Near to the base of the slope they were almost continuously shooting at the Scarrogs to keep them at bay. Anxiously, Milly looked at the wall ahead of them. Not far now. The circle of Scarrogs had broken and there was a gap ahead where they could make a break for it.

Again Charlie fired the red beam at an aggressive Scarrog that got too close, but this time he noticed the red was fainter than before. The Scarrog went down, but it wasn't dead. Painfully, the creature was able to wobble away.

'I'm running low,' he called to Milly in desperation. He tried firing at the nearest Scarrog but the beam was pale and didn't even reach his intended target.

For another minute Milly kept the Scarrogs at bay with almost continuous firing, until her beam turned faint too. Desperately, they looked towards the wall ahead of them. Tod, Sam and all their friends were standing on the stones, shouting encouragement. But the Scarrogs had realised that Milly and Charlie had stopped firing and became bolder in their attacks. In one seething mass of bodies, they surged forward, scurrying fast and buzzing with fresh zeal. They sensed a weakened enemy.

'RUN!' shouted Milly. She and Charlie threw caution to the winds and, heading for the gap in the circle, sprinted for the wall and safety.

Sam was standing on the stone wall and jumping up and down with excitement when he realised there was a problem. When the Scarrogs suddenly charged after Charlie and Milly, he jumped down off the wall and raced to help his distressed friends. Charlie was leading the race, so Sam sprinted past him and on to Milly where he skidded into a quick turnaround, grabbing her as he went. Gaining speed again, Sam raced back to the wall with Milly in his arms.

Looking back over Sam's shoulder, as he sped back to the wall, Milly realised that Charlie would not make it to safety. The instant Sam dropped her, she screamed at Tod. 'Your jetpack! Give me your jetpack quickly!'

The rocket boy had realised that Milly's jetpack was now a weapon, so he snatched at the buckle round his chest and, slipping the straps off his shoulders, flung his jetpack to Milly. It only took her a second to fit it to her chest and heave out the tube. Twisting the lever, she was back on the wall and generating the deadly red beam.

Fear made Charlie race quicker than he had ever run before. At any moment he expected to be hauled down by the pursuing Scarrogs. He was gasping for breath, feet pounding towards the wall, when Milly's red beam shot over his head and he heard a scream from close behind as a Scarrog was hit. More screams came from behind him as the red beam moved from side to side picking out victims at random. Then suddenly he felt himself raised up and carried aloft by hands so fast he could barely see them. The wall was close by and he felt the lurch as Sam, holding him fast, jumped it in a single stride.

The Scarrogs milled around in front of the wall, buzzing louder than ever. A few even tried to clamber over, but the deadly red ray knocked them off and sought out any that came too close. Realising the game was up, the Scarrogs soon retreated to a distance where their buzzing was nothing more than a faint hum.

The transformation of the jetpacks from rocket to weapon attracted all the attention. Everyone could see that the battle for survival against the Scarrogs would change dramatically in future. Even with just three of the rocket jetpacks, they could fight off the Scarrogs and even chase them back to the swamp.

The excitement of the discovery seemed to make everybody talk at once, so Samsa and Charlie were in demand to translate question after question from the Thinkers and Waterlanders alike.

'What's in the building?'

'Are there any more jetpacks there?'

'Did you understand the voice?

'What did it say?'

'Who built the building?'

Eventually, Milly put her hands over her ears and Charlie jumped onto the wall again and shouted loudly to quieten everybody down. 'We will tell you everything we learnt, in time, but there are too many people here right now. We must speak with your leaders. They will pass on any knowledge we have about the building. But I can tell you this,' and here he shouted as loudly as he could. 'That doorway is the entrance to a huge cavern which has been hollowed out inside the mountain. It contains the history and the secrets of the ancients who came here when cavemen roamed the earth.'

Gasps of astonishment fluttered around the crowd gathered before him. More questions filled the air, but Charlie raised his hands and jumped down from the wall, exhausted by his long adventure.

'Come on,' said Milly, taking his hand. 'We need to get some rest.'

13

RUMBLINGS

The following morning, they awoke to a strange sensation. The ground beneath their hut was shaking.

The noise of small stones falling from nearby rocks made the children jump up and hurry outside to see what was going on.

They found Merfan, the leader of the Thinkers, standing by the wall. He looked worried.

'We have had many such shakes in the past.' he said. 'Some are just tremors, but other times, rocks from the mountain fall down and crash among us.'

He looked anxiously at the high mountain above the village. They could see the trees shaking on the mountainside.

'Look,' said Charlie, pointing to where the black lake with its surrounding swamp was rapidly disappearing. It looked as though a giant plug had been pulled out of the ground, draining all the water into a hole in the earth.

Sam turned to Merfan and asked him anxiously, 'Has this happened before?'

'It has,' the old man replied with a solemn nod. 'And it is happening more frequently. Every time the water slips away as you see, taking everything with it, even the Scarrogs. After a few days of nothing, the lake returns, and so do the Scarrogs, bigger and more aggressive than before.' He shook his head sadly. 'I fear for our future in this land.' His face looked strained and lined and he seemed to shrink with despair.

Charlie stared at the land that stretched down to the swamp. An idea occurred to him. 'You said that the lake and the Scarrogs disappear for a few days.' he said, looking at Merfan.

The old man nodded his head in confirmation.

'Then we can safely go over to the building,' said Charlie, turning excitedly to the others. 'Because if the Scarrogs are gone, what's to stop us?'

'And then what?' said the old man with a shrug. 'What could we learn?'

Charlie's excitement levels grew steadily as he explained.

'One of the incredible features of the building is the way the ancients enabled all their information to be translated into any language. The Thinkers and the Waterlanders can listen to the history and the rest of the information quite easily. All you have to do is talk in your own language to a machine and it learns how to speak to you.'

The others looked at him in disbelief.

'It's true!' added Milly. 'We tried it and it works.'

Bredon, who had come to join the small group, picked up on Charlie's mood and took the initiative. 'We must go to the buildings now,' he said, making a fist in the air. 'The Scarrogs are going with the waters. We must see how much we can learn in the time before they return.'

A murmur of great anticipation spread around the group. More of the villagers were joining in and soon a great buzz of enthusiasm began to spread. They were all keen to see and learn of the wonders the ancients had left in store.

'A team,' said Milly to Merfan and Bredon. 'You can't have everybody rushing over and crowding into the building all at once, it'll be chaos. You need to be organised.'

It was three days before the waters returned to the swamp. When it did, the Scarrogs emerged from it and walked slowly around its edges. They appeared groggy, as if the journey with the waters had exhausted them, and made no attempt to attack the people hurrying to and from the ancient building.

Nevertheless Sam, Charlie and Milly stood guard with their new weapons at the ready.

Tod had spent much of his time helping the Thinkers and Waterlanders to learn from the books and pictures they saw in the cavernous room. Sometimes Singer went with him, but she soon found all the information hard to absorb. One evening, after a meal, she told the others how surprised she was at Tod's excited concentration in the cavern. 'He just wants to know everything there is to know about the ancients,' she said. 'I always thought of Tod as a bit of a clown! You know how cheerful and happy-go-lucky he can be, but I've never seen him so serious. If you want to know about the people who lived here in those times, just ask Tod.'

So they did. 'How did the ancients get here?' asked Sam, when Tod made one of his rare appearances back at the village. 'And what happened to them?'

Tod gave his usual toothy grin and sighed. 'It's a long, unbelievable story,' he said, settling himself down. As the eager faces waited for him to go on, he knew he had them hooked. 'Basically, all the people who live behind the hedge are descended from the people who crashed here a very long time ago. In the history section of the time book, a man called Ergo tells the story. There's a picture of him on the screen and behind him pictures of the stars and another world... It's amazing.'

'Ergo must be the man we saw when we first explored the building,' said Charlie. 'But why did they come here?'

'The planet they call Zendora was old and dying, so they built huge ships to travel across space and find new planets on which to settle. The ship that came here was called the Enjin. When it tried to land, something went wrong; it came down too fast and crashed. At first, the occupants weren't too worried because this planet was just what they wanted. It was much like the planet they came from, with plenty of water and forests and mountains, and a climate that was generally warm and comfortable.

'But other creatures existed here - primitive man! Warlike and vicious, vast numbers of them began to attack the Zendorans. You see...' Tod leaned forward, his eyes blazing as he told the story, 'the Zendorans had no weapons. They had never needed them. These people were a peaceful breed, seeking only a place to live and prosper. But what they found here...'

Tod shook his head.

'Our friendly ancestors!' said Sam with a resigned shrug.

Tod continued. 'They lost many of their friends before taking refuge in the remains of their ship. From there, they looked out through windows at a strange new world that had suddenly turned hostile.'

'What happened then?' asked Milly, eager for more.

'The ancients used the Enjin, rebuilt it. They couldn't make a ship, but Ergo spoke of something called an SES power unit that supplied all the energy they needed.'

Singer frowned. 'What's an *SES power unit*?'

Tod frowned and furrowed his brow. 'It stands for Sun Energy Simulator, I don't know how it works, well, not yet I don't.' Then he smiled happily again and added hopefully, 'But I will soon.'

He paused to remember the thread of his story, then carried on. 'They used the SES to create a giant bubble of something they called *light enriched zenna molecules*, which means that once it was in place nothing could enter into the bubble. Then they grew a bio mechanical hedge all around it, with special openings, so they could explore the new world whenever they wanted, but get back in and be safe if they had to.'

'That must be how we got in,' said Singer.

'Through one of those entrances, yes,' said Tod. 'For centuries, they watched mankind grow.' Tod almost began to laugh as he spoke. 'They've witnessed almost every major event of civilisation, but always managed to keep themselves a complete secret, hidden inside their bubble... But things were changing. Men were growing more clever.'

'Where did the snakeheads come from?' asked Milly. 'Surely they didn't bring them with them.'

Tod raised a finger as though he had been waiting for this question.

'Apparently the bubble created its own problems. It trapped a lot of native species within its boundaries who couldn't escape, so carried on living here. Ergo said that a combination of radiation surges and separate development created rival species, which competed for everything within the bubble. Even the people who arrived on the ship formed themselves into separate groups. Some people wanted to live permanently in the Enjin and have control of the power plant, so they threw out all the rest.'

'They must be the Robes!' said Charlie.

'And the Dome is the old ship,' added Sam, stunned by the sudden realisation. 'What happened to the others?'

'They left the valley and went off in all directions.'

'The Minlings are terrified of the Robes and work for them all the time,' said Milly. 'They must have been one group.'

'And the Waterlanders settled in another valley,' added Sam.

'And the Thinkers went even further but couldn't get back to mix with any of the others,' said Singer. 'That must be what Ergo meant by separate development.'

Tod looked thoughtful for a moment 'There's so much more to find out. The Thinkers and the Waterlanders are learning a lot, every day. There are drawings and information on how to build practically anything. These ancient people were very advanced and everything they knew was written down in these machines and stored in the cavern. The only thing missing is weapons; for some reason there are no guns or deadly ray machines in the store. So there is a problem.'

Milly realised what it was. 'The Scarrogs come back and we only have three rocket jetpacks, which we don't want to leave behind, so, after we go home, they cannot hold the Scarrogs off forever.'

'Exactly,' added Charlie. 'Also, we know they run out of energy in a prolonged battle and they take time to re-energise,' added Charlie. 'It's about two hours before they can be used again. 'So what do we do when the Scarrogs realise we are defenceless?'

'I have a proposal,' said Tod, lapsing into silent thought. The children had never seen him look so solemn, so they remained quiet and waited for him to continue.

'The Thinkers have found a map which shows a path up the mountain and back to the Waterlanders valley. They can all escape from this valley, but only to face the Robes. They don't want to leave the secrets of the ancient building behind, which means they need to return with weapons to fight off the Scarrogs. Remember, I told you of a room in the Dome which was full of rocket jetpacks that now turns out to be a room full of weapons as well. The jetpacks have been gathering dust for generations and have been long forgotten by the Robes. If we are going to go home and leave the Waterlanders and the Thinkers safe, we need those weapons.'

'How do we get them?' asked Sam.

'We declare war on the Robes,' said Tod solemnly.

There was a moment of stunned silence as the others all stopped to take in what Tod had just said. Getting to his feet, Tod took a deep breath and continued.

'I will lead an army of Waterlanders and Thinkers

over the mountains and attack the Dome. It will be a surprise attack and we will go straight to that storage room and capture the weapons.' He paused and, drawing himself to his full height, declared, 'I want to liberate the descendants of the people of Zendora and lead them to freedom and a new life, dedicated to learning the knowledge left as their inheritance.' His speech ended with him shouting out his message across the valley with his arm held high and a mad gleam in his eye.

It was a bold speech and the children looked at each other in surprise. They had never seen Tod act like this before and they burst out laughing.

'I'm not sure you have all the qualities of a leader,' said Sam. 'No offence, but you are known as the mad rocket boy and you don't even speak their language.'

Tod looked at him and gave him a toothy grin. 'I have been learning the language every day. Samsa is with me all the time and she speaks all languages. I am finding it surprisingly easy. I think I have a natural talent and, actually, the languages are very similar which is not surprising since they all came from the same ancestors.'

'Have you told Merfan, Bredon and the others of your plan?' asked Singer. She did not like fighting and felt very nervous about Tod being in charge of anything, let alone an army.

'No, but I am about to break the good news to them.' He gave them a little nod and, tightening his lips, set off with a determined stride to the hut where the leaders were gathered.

The children gathered together in a huddle to discuss Tod's idea. Milly considered it to be the only option and, although they were worried about all the things that could go wrong, the others had to agree with her.

Reluctantly, they followed Tod over to the main hut and arrived just in time to hear him declare, in a loud and strident voice, 'We will descend from the hills like avenging demons and fight our way to victory. We will reclaim the Dome and bring the knowledge of our ancestors to its home in the old ship, so that the glory of their memory will return and all the people will be united!'

To the astonishment of the children, all those in the hut stood up and cheered madly. Some of them were chanting.

'Tod! Tod! Tod!'

Red Headband, Samsa's father and leader of the Waterlander warriors, joined them in the doorway. In his hand he held the spear he always kept with him. 'We have a warlord who can return us to our lands and restore the glory of our past,' he said with a broad smile on his face. They could see the light of battle already gleaming in his eyes.

Moments later the Waterlanders and Thinkers left the hut, enthused by Tod's speech, and rushed to spread the word that they were all leaving the valley to overcome the Robes.

'They've all gone stark raving bonkers,' said Sam

looking after them.

'And who do you think the front line troops will be?' mused Charlie.

'Us, of course!' groaned Milly. 'Oh well, they're our weapons and I'm not letting mine out of my sight. The three of us will blast our way in and just hope that the Robes haven't found the room were the jetpacks are stored. As for a surprise attack, how do you take all these warriors over miles of land without the Robes knowing what's coming?'

14

THE EXODUS

There was a new atmosphere in the valley as Tod and Red Headband organised their troops.

The children were always on guard duty, standing near the stone wall with the tubes of their jetpacks extended, ready to fire at any Scarrogs who came too near.

The Waterlanders meanwhile gathered stones to build a bridge over to the path. It started above the cave where the slope from the Waterlanders' valley ended. The mountain walls around the cave were sheer rock that was impossible to climb, so the first stage of the journey involved building a staircase to reach the path.

'To think the start of the path out of here had been right under their noses for generations,' said Charlie as he helped to build the stairway by dumping a large stone on top of the pile.

'I can understand that,' said Singer standing back and looking up the mountain. 'You would never know it was there; in fact I'm still not sure it is. That is a very old map and I can't see any sign of a tunnel.'

But it was there, and Tod and Sam climbed up to the cave entrance and gazed back over the valley.

It was a point high above the valley and they could see for miles. The swamp in the distance still had Scarrogs roaming around it and a crowd of them had gathered by the stone wall. The valley stretched out before them and in the distance more villages could be seen. A distant river flowed towards them, meandering its way across the valley to the swamp. But the scene that drew their attention was the crowd of Thinkers and Waterlanders milling around in the village.

'Look at that, Tod,' said Sam. 'You appear to be the warlord of a mighty army.

Tod gulped. 'I hadn't realised just how many villages there are in the valley,' he said. 'They must have deserted all their homes ready for the journey.'

As soon as they climbed down to the village Tod called a meeting of the elders and the children and told them what to expect on the journey ahead.

'We set out immediately and nobody must be left behind. Take only food and drink because we will be moving fast.' He then reassured the leaders that there was no way the ancient building of knowledge would be abandoned. 'On the contrary,' he said, 'the building was designed by the ancient ones for our benefit and we will reap the benefit in the future.'

'Or rather, the Thinkers will reap the benefits,' said Singer with a frown. 'The rest of us will be going back to the orphanage.' She realised the only way to help the people was to rid the valley of the Scarrogs and the only way to do that was for them to return with weapons and those weapons were hidden in the Dome. But the way Tod had escalated the problem with a call to arms and war with the Robes unsettled her enormously.

'Of course,' said Tod with a dismissive gesture with his hand. 'We want to do what's best for the people. But now we must get everyone moving.' Turning to the leaders, he saw they were waiting for instructions and behind them the anxious faces of the crowd told him they needed some reassurance. So, holding his hands up high he roared as loud as he could. 'We need to leave this valley now and seek out the Dome, but we will return, liberated, and live in peace once more.' A great roar of approval met his words and the crowd surged forwards, keen to be on the move.

It took several hours to get the inhabitants of the valley onto the path and moving slowly up the mountain. It led them high into the mountains and when it came to a sudden end they all scouted around for the entrance to a cave. It was one of the warriors who found it. The undergrowth had grown over the entrance and it took a lot of pulling and breaking of branches before it appeared.

The rocket jetpacks had an adjustment that turned the rays into a bright torch. With his pack strapped to his chest, Tod led the way into the cave, filling the tunnel with light as he went.

It was colder in the tunnel but it was a large straight passage with a high roof that seemed to be taking them in the right direction. The light on the jetpack was invaluable. Earthquakes had caused some problems with the tunnel walls; boulders and small rocks littered the floor. Above them, the light picked out sparking reflections from the eyes of hundreds of tiny bats who were roosting there, squeaking in annoyance at the unexpected disturbance.

When the first people reached the other side they stopped to marvel at the view, but Tod kept urging them to move on down the hillside. The population of the Thinkers' valley turned out to be much bigger than he had thought, so he gave orders to Red Headband to go on ahead of the crowd and find a place for an overnight stop.

By the time the main army reached the bottom of the hill, Red Headband and his warriors had prepared and secured a large clearing in the woods. When the main mass of people arrived at the camp site there were fires already lit. The travellers shared their provisions and blankets with one another. It was an exhausted band that settled down for a night out in the open.

The next morning, Red Headband and his men were up very early and set off down the hillside to prepare a camp for the next night's stop. The leader of the warriors reckoned that it would take just one more day after that to reach the lake and the old Waterlanders village.

'Be careful and keep a sharp look out for Robes,' called out Sam as he watched them go.

Nobody could keep to the path when the main group set out later on. There were just too many people so everyone made their own way down as best they could. When they came to a grassy plateau, Tod held up his hand and shouted for them all to take a rest. He was concerned that the women and children were getting left behind and he believed everyone would be safer if they stuck together.

The children from Mercy Hall gathered together with Tod to take stock of the situation when they heard a tick-tock noise coming from overhead.

'There you are,' shrieked a familiar voice. 'The trouble I've had finding you lot. Where've you been?' Batty was agitated and shouted as loudly as she could.

They all looked up and smiled.

'Robert made me come,' said Batty. 'I've had to fly high over mountains and I've been frightened by hawks and snakeheads. Even Jangles didn't know where you were. Oh, the trouble you've caused me!'

Batty dropped down, settling herself on Sam's shoulder and looking around. 'My, what a lot of people you have here? Where are you all going?' The bird didn't wait for an answer but carried on talking. 'By the way, there's a Waterlander fellow with a red band round his head fighting with a load of Snakeheads just over the next ridge.'

'What!' screeched Tod. 'Where?'

Milly jumped to her feet. 'Lead the way you silly bird,' she shouted. 'Go on, fly.'

Sam pushed the bird into the air and grabbed his

jetpack.

'To the rescue,' shouted Tod to all the people around him. 'Charge!' He raced to edge of the plateau at the exact point were Batty was fluttering and launched himself down the hill. The Thinkers and Waterlanders responded quickly to his cry and hundreds of them grabbed spears and sticks and charged down the hill after him.

At the bottom of the hill, Red Headband and his Waterlanders had been surprised and overcome by a band of Snakeheads. Some of the Waterlanders were pinned to the ground and others were being dragged away by the Snakesheads with their hands shackled and ropes around their necks.

Batty was the first to arrive. Giving out an unearthly scream, she swooped low to dive-bomb a large Snakehead who had a Waterlander in his grasp and was throttling the life out of him. The Snakehead dropped his victim in surprise and ducked as Batty's shrill cries blasted his ears. He threw his scaly hands in the air to defend himself from the attacker but Batty had moved on and was hovering over another Snakehead, scratching at his head and screaming again. There was a pause in the fighting as several Snakeheads hurled spears at the attacking bird. Then the noise made by the army of people charging down the hill attracted their attention.

When the Thinkers and the Waterlanders saw the Snakesheads attacking their friends a great cry of fury went up which built into a crescendo of noise as the small army, which included women and children, raced into battle. For a frozen moment in time the Snakeheads stared at the mob running down the hill towards them. Then they abandoned their prisoners and fled. The scaly creatures threw caution to the wind and charged away down the hillside crashing into small bushes and banging into trees. A small band of Waterlanders might look a tasty capture for their tribe but a green skinned army was a different matter.

When the Snakeheads disappeared into the forest at the bottom of the hill, the chasing crowd stopped and gave a great cheer. They were still excited and congratulating each other when they returned to re-join their leaders.

At the end of the day a new camp was established and the children and the elders sat down to plan for the future. It was the actions of Batty that they talked about first.

'What bravery!' said Bredon, enormously impressed with the way the bird had fearlessly attacked a Snakehead.

'She should be awarded a medal,' said Tinkamus, an elder with a shrivelled face and a twinkle in his eyes.

'What sort of a medal?' asked Milly, equally surprised by Batty's sudden bravery. It was something the bird had never done before; in fact, Batty generally went out of her way to avoid danger.

'I have in mind the order of the Golden Star,' said

Tinkamus. 'In the history of the ancients, which I have been studying, they awarded this medal to some of their people for outstanding courage. I believe this is something that needs to be re-instated for the new world we are about to build. With your approval I will have one made, to be presented to Batty at a later and more convenient time.'

Everyone nodded in agreement.

Milly went to talk to Batty, who was perched on the low branch of a nearby tree and appeared to be sleeping. 'Are you awake Batty?' she asked gently.

The bird opened one eye and peered at her. 'I am now,' she said grumpily.

Milly couldn't resist stretching out an arm to stroke Batty on her back and realised that the bird was still trembling. 'I didn't know you could scream like that?' she said.

'It's given me a very sore throat,' croaked Batty. 'It's not something I shall ever do again. I don't know what came over me, I much prefer to be a coward and fly away from danger,' she sniffed and looked quite miserable.

'Well you were very brave and we are all very proud of you.'

'They threw spears at me,' Batty grumbled, then closed her eyes.

Milly stroked Batty again and returned to join in the conversation with the leaders.

The following morning found Sam sitting in a tree close to the old Waterlander village. He had used his great speed to run ahead of the main army to spy on the Robes at the lake.

A noise disturbed him as he waited impatiently in his hiding place. It was a crackling noise like branches breaking and it came from above him. The noise got louder; something was coming towards him, rapidly and crashing through the trees.

Finally his tree started shaking but the noise stopped. He tensed his body, expecting an attack. A leaf dropped into his lap and he jerked his head up to see what had made it fall. Two brown eyes peered down at him from high up in the tree. Then a hairy face popped out and smiled.

'Hello,' said Mo. 'Did I surprise you?'

Sam sighed with relief. 'You did, you sounded like a whole herd of Baboons crashing through the trees like that. I'm supposed to be hiding.' He turned to look at the village but there was no sign that the Robes knew he was there.

'Sorry,' said Mo and he eased himself down to squat alongside him in the tree. Moments later the tree shook again and Flo, Bee and Bo noisily dropped down to his branch and beamed at him.

'Tell them to be quiet,' said Sam.

Mo apologised again and grunted at his family.

'I'm glad you found me,' whispered Sam and he told them of their adventures in the valley of the Thinkers and the plans they had to attack the Dome.

The tree shook yet again and to Sam's immense surprise about twenty smaller monkeys dropped out of the tree above him and squabbled noisily over sitting places on the branch.

Sam covered his face with his hands in despair. 'Where did all these fellows come from?' he hissed at Mo.

'We found them living in the forest. They told us you were back. Good spies they are.'

'Hopefully we won't be here for long,' said Sam. 'We have to get back to the orphanage as soon as possible.'

The chimpanzee family muttered and grunted amongst themselves for a while then Mo looked sadly at Sam. 'We've made a lot of friends here,' he said. 'I know we said we would come back with you but we like it here. Would you mind if we stayed here. We'll always be grateful to you for helping us escape.'

'Of course you can,' replied Sam. 'But right now, I have to be quiet and stay hidden. Can you please move these jabbering things to another tree?'

Mo put a finger to his lips to show he understood the problem and slowly the chimpanzees and the other monkeys melted away into the forest.

Later in the day Sam watched as busy Robes hurried back and forth, loading their boats lined up on the shoreline. The Robe giving the orders stood on a mound close by with three other Robes around him. An orange gown hung loosely round his scrawny body and skinny feet wrapped in dirty sandals poked out below. As he turned to look nervously at the forest, Sam saw a face like a hungry rat with watery eyes and thin lips.

Later, Tod told him that the Robe's name was Bulkrit. He was the man responsible for making Old Barking Mad their King.

'They know we're coming and they are frightened,' thought Sam, peering through the leaves of his hiding place. 'They are getting ready to leave.'

The Robes loaded up the boats and forced the captured Waterlanders to push the vessels into the water. Bulkrit was the last to leave. He stood in the boat and stared back at the village with a scowl on his face as his boat moved off.

With the Robes some way offshore, Sam clambered down from the tree and wandered casually out to the beach. Standing in water that lapped around his feet, he waved slowly at the departing boats.

'You!' screeched Bulkrit at the boy on the edge of the lake. 'You're one of the creatures from behind the hedge. I'll see you never return there. You will die in this land!'

Sam hoped that seeing him defenceless would tempt the departing boat to return and try to capture him. He desperately wanted the army of Waterlanders to arrive before the Robes left. For a moment he thought the enraged Robe would do as he wished, but suddenly Bulkrit straightened up and stared over his head. Turning, Sam saw the advance party of the Waterlander army streaming out of the forest. Running, yelling and waving their spears, the warriors ran wildly to join him on the beach.

Some of them splashed into the water to chase the boats, but Sam called them back. Waterlanders lived mainly by fishing and were brilliant swimmers, but the Robes' boats were gathering speed and were obviously going to escape. Sam knew there would be time to catch them soon enough...

Throughout the day the Thinker and Waterlander families arrived at the village and settled down in the huts and on the beach for a well-earned rest.

Warlord Tod however insisted the leaders join him in the main hut to listen to the plan he had drawn up for the attack on the Dome. They listened carefully to the details that involved a three pronged attack, leaving the women and children in the village guarded by a small force of Waterlanders.

The first change to Tod's plan came when the women and children refused to be left behind.

'But we can't have women and children in a battle,' he said to Bredon, who brought him the news.

'May I remind you,' said Bredon, 'that you are a child yourself and two of your friends are girls. The women and children are very determined to come and nobody will be able to stop them.'

Tod sighed. 'Oh, all right then, I shall amend the plan and use them as best I can.' He thought for a moment then smiled. 'Yes,' he said. 'A diversion! They will make a perfect diversion. Kindly pass on the information that I require all the females to dress as their fathers and brothers and to carry spears.'

Preparations for the coming assault on the Dome were already underway. Carts were loaded with tools, ropes, axes, saws and spears, while others carried provisions and water. The Robes had taken all the Waterlander boats across the lake, so the following day the entire population started walking around the lake to leave the valley.

The only easy way out of the valley was on the other side of the lake where a passage through the rocks led down to a cave where a waterfall hid the entrance. The key to their success, according to Tod, was the strategic use of the three jetpack weapons they had. 'These ray guns are brilliant,' he said. 'But there are only three of them and they do run out of energy. We must use them judiciously if we want them to last. Surprise is essential; the Robes do not know that we have such deadly weapons, and they may be complacent, believing we have no chance of winning.'

The first flashpoint was likely to be the narrow passage out of the waterfall cave. At this point a few determined Robes with spears could hold up the entire army for a long time. But to their relief, they found no resistance there or anywhere else on the journey.

That afternoon they arrived at the river that flowed out of the forest and down to the Dome. Here Tod split his forces into two distinct units. Red Headband took the first unit, a strong force of well-armed warriors, deep into the forest. Their job was to cross the river at the point before it reached the Dome. Sam and Milly went with them wearing the weapons they hoped would play a major part in the attack. The second unit remained behind, awaiting further instructions.

Just before nightfall Tod, Singer, Charlie and the rest of the army drew close to the Dome. The large building stuck out of the ground like a giant elaborate thumb. The river flowed towards it then swung around to pass behind. To attack the Dome, the army had to cross the river. On the opposite bank a crowd of Robes had gathered and the two sides exchanged insults by shouting across the water.

'You are bunch of weak, yellow bellied farmers!' roared a Robe.

'Flee to the forest while you have a chance,' replied a Waterlander with an angry yet confident voice.

'Robes will always beat Waterlanders,' boasted another Robe.

'Wait until the morning,' howled a Thinker, jumping up and down in a gesture that looked almost like a jolly dance. 'You'll be sorry when we cross the river.'

15

THE BATTLE FOR THE DOME

While the hubbub of noise carried on across the river, nightfall started to cast long shadows. Carrying out his plans with a great thoroughness, Tod gathered together a select group of people hand-picked for an important mission. Their success depended on silently swimming across the river under cover of darkness and making for the Dome.

Before their departure, Tod took Singer to one side. 'Remember,' he said, in hushed, conspiratorial tones, 'the women and children are to be dressed as if they are warriors. The Robes won't be able to tell the difference from across the river. Your job is to provide a diversion, not to fight.'

Just before dawn, Tod and ten men slipped away from the main group and headed down to the bank. At Tod's command, the ten Waterlanders slid silently into the river and swam underwater to the other side. Tod had told them of a small door behind the Dome which he promised would be open to them at daybreak. Until that moment, they were to stay hidden in the water.

Meanwhile, Tod had a special job to do.

He went as far away from the main grouping as possible before strapping the jetpack onto his back and setting it into rocket mode. He wanted to approach the Dome from a good height under cover of darkness, so as not to be seen or heard when crossing the river. Although he put on a brave appearance in front of his friends and the Waterlanders, his legs were wobbling with fright as he prepared to take off in the dark. Fortunately, the Dome gave off enough light for it to be seen clearly and, gritting his teeth, he took to the air and powered his way towards it. Landing was always a problem for Tod, particularly at night, but his nerves made him especially careful tonight, and he managed to land with barely more than a slight clatter.

When he was certain he hadn't been seen, he bent down and opened up a string fastener on top of the jetpack; inside was a small storage area where he kept a few personal things. He slid his hand down to the bottom of the jetpack and pulled out a neatly folded orange gown. He shook it out and looked at it with a satisfied smile on his face. Then he slipped it over his head and shoulders and down over his waist. Standing up straight he twirled around and decided it was a good fit; he could pass for a junior Robe.

Carrying his jetpack under his arm, Tod left the roof by a door that led to a winding staircase and found a hive of activity inside. He didn't meet anybody on the first three floors, but as he got nearer to the centre, Robes were hurrying or running in every direction. He nodded at a few of them as they passed, but nobody took much notice of him. After all, he looked just like one of them, so why should they bother? He smiled to himself with relief and made his way to the ground floor at the rear of the Dome.

The staircase leading to the very bottom of the Dome was near to the back door. Tod was hoping that when he let the Waterlanders in it would be very quiet down there. It was important not to have anyone raise the alarm before he reached the storeroom way down in the depths.

The back door was halfway down a long corridor. It was bolted when he arrived, but at least there were no Robes guarding it. Now was the time to remove his disguise, so he hid it in his jetpack and strapped the unit on in weapons mode.

He listened intently for any approaching footsteps, but there was nothing. After another quick look down each of the nearest corridors, he grasped the

cold, metal handle and yanked it down. The door opened with a harsh scrape that made him pause for a second, fearful he may have been heard. No sound followed, so he pushed the door a little further and peered outside.

The day was brightening just enough for him to see over the river flowing nearby. A ripple in the water caught his eye and he stared at it hopefully. Then, the curly black hair of a Waterlander emerged, quickly followed by another and another. Seconds later his ten friends were gliding through the water towards him. The first person out of the water was Lazrus, a big man with a wide smile, who wore only a black tunic fastened round his waist. None of the warriors wasted any time in joining Tod in the doorway.

'No talking,' he ordered. 'Follow me.'

They got to the staircase at the very back of the Dome and Tod led his men down six flights of stairs without incident. Very few of the Robes ever went down there and now he knew why. The information from the building of knowledge had told him that the Dome was the actual ship the ancients had crashed in when they arrived on the planet. The front had sunk deep into the soft ground, and it was here the jetpacks were stored. If the people with knowledge of the weapons had perished in the crash, then anyone who came across them wouldn't know what they were. Tod had only found them by accident.

Damage to the ship could be seen everywhere. Great cracks had split the walls and holes in some ceilings revealed masses of coloured wires hanging down. It was obvious nobody from the Dome ever came down this far. Dust was thick everywhere and they left footprints with every step they took. In fact, it was the footprints and disturbed dust that Tod had left the first time he'd been down to the room that showed them where to go this time round.

'This is it!' shouted Tod in triumph as he found the right door and he ushered his men inside. It was empty, but Tod walked to an old wardrobe in the corner and heaved it to one side to reveal a small door set in the wall behind it. 'I hid behind this wardrobe once,' he said remembering the day he escaped from the Robes.

A passageway behind the door led to another room that was stacked with rocket jetpacks. 'Everyone grab a jetpack and line up alongside me,' ordered Tod.

The Waterlanders had watched Tod use the jetpack as a flying machine and a weapon, so it was easy for them to copy his actions as he demonstrated how it worked. His men lined up against one wall and Tod checked that they all had a jetpack firmly strapped to their chests and its tube extended in stun mode. Each Waterlander could hook two jetpacks over each elbow and still work the one strapped to their chest. It was awkward, but as Tod said, 'It won't be for long. Now we have to blast our way out of here so, let's go.'

It took them a lot longer than Tod had planned to climb back up to ground level. They met a few

Robes on the way and dealt with them quickly enough with a blast of the yellow ray. Finally they reached the ground floor and burst out of the main door with all their weapons at the ready.

Singer had her troops up early, chopping down trees and dragging them to the river bank. She was following instructions and made the camp look a hive of activity. On the far side of the river more and more Robes gathered to watch them. Most of them carried spears and were organised as a fighting force, but they were not very concerned. They could see that they outnumbered the Waterlander army, who did not have any boats and could only cross the river by swimming.

Singer ordered all the people, including the women and children to take to the water and swim over to the opposite bank. A great cheer went up from the watching Robes as the tree trunks were pushed out and the Waterlander army floated their makeshift wooden rafts across the river. Slowly the army drifted down the river. Swimming frantically, they edged slowly to the opposite bank. The Robes walked along the river bank to keep level with them and taunted them to come ashore and fight.

It was the moment Singer had been waiting for.

Turning, she stopped to wave to a solitary figure on the hill behind her. It was Samsa, whose job it was to signal to Red Headband and the Waterlanders that all the Robes were busy watching the women and children cross the river. Samsa picked up a green flag on a long handle and waved it to and fro.

Red Headband and his warriors, having made it to the other side of the river, gathered in the forest behind the Robes. The road to the Dome was clear, but for a few Robes heading down the causeway that led to the front door. They were too few in number to cause a problem to Red Headband and his men, who had instructions to race as fast as they could to the front entrance of the Dome once the signal was given. One of his men had climbed a tree to watch the hill in the distance. He could just see the solitary figure of Samsa standing there. When she lifted the flag and waved it, he shouted down to the waiting Waterlanders; the signal had been given.

As quietly as they could, Red Headband and his men scampered out of the forest and started the dash across open ground to the entrance of the Dome. Sam was leading the race, keeping himself to a steady pace so the others could keep up, but Milly was left behind by the speed and enthusiasm of the warriors.

The Waterlander army in the water was watching for the signal as well. As soon as Samsa waved the flag, they all turned round and started to push the tree trunks back to the bank they had just left, as if they were too frightened to carry on. A great cheer went up from the Robes, who began to roar with laughter.

Tod and his men were gasping with exhaustion when they burst out into the open air just in time to see Samsa on the hill waving her green flag and Red Headband's men heading towards them from the forest.

The charging warriors saw Tod and his men emerge from the Dome, carrying weapons for them, and gave out a great cheer.

The Robes on the bank of the river heard the noise and they all turned round together. They were stunned to see a great band of Waterlanders racing towards the Dome. The leaders amongst them called for the armed Robes to ready their spears and return to defend the Dome.

Realising they had been tricked, and that a force of Waterlanders were now blocking their way back to the Dome still caused little concern. The charging Waterlanders were outnumbered and the rest of the army were on the wrong side of the river.

While Sam and Milly had been waiting in the forest they had taken their two jetpack weapons and shown every Waterlander how to use them. Every member of their band wanted to get their hands on their own weapon and, as soon as they reached the front of the Dome and met up with Tod's men, the first twenty men snatched up a spare jetpack and strapped it onto their chests.

'Take up lines of battle,' ordered Tod, feeling

pleased with himself. So far everything was going to plan.

Ten of the Waterlanders spread out and lined up with Tod in front of the Dome. Each one had the tube of his weapon extended and pointing at the approaching Robes. The others, led by Red Headband, appeared to run back towards the forest.

When the charging Robes got near to the Dome they found a single line of ten Waterlanders spread out in front of them. They had expected their enemy to bunch together and take the charge head on. To line up as they did was unexpected and made the Robes slow their pace.

Bulkrit himself had been at the front of the charge but now he stopped to allow his spearmen to run past him. He was suspicious that something was wrong; when faced with an overwhelming force in the past, the Waterlanders had always run away. Now, a line of ten men awaited the charge without showing any signs of fear.

'Now!' called Tod, as the charging Robes got close.

Yellow beams streaked into the ranks of the Robes. The effect was devastating. Every Robe that was hit, dropped like a stone and lay motionless on the ground.

Bulkrit looked on in amazement and didn't know how to react. As far as he knew, a strange new weapon had killed his people. None of them appeared wounded and none were groaning, they just lay crumpled on the ground.

Panic made all the Robes still standing turn and flee. They did so with screams of fear, trampling over each other in their haste to get away. At first they ran back to the river but realising there was no escape that way, they tried to dash for the forest. However, Red Headband had led the rest of his men in a long semicircle with the intention of surrounding the Robes and preventing any escape.

Yellow beams shot into the ranks of the Robes from all directions until Tod called for a cease fire. By then the Robes had nowhere to go and they all sat on the ground, exhausted and defeated and pleading for surrender.

Sam and Milly joined Tod at the Dome. He was showing his old toothy grin that spread from ear to ear. 'We did it,' he said gleefully.

'What do we do now?' asked Milly, pleased that

the Robes had surrendered and nobody had been killed, but worried about their next move.

'I am about to make the most important speech in my life,' said Tod solemnly. 'When all those Robes lying on the ground have recovered, go and tell Bulkrit to lead his people into the Great Hall and make sure Red Headband and his men don't let any of them escape.'

'Where are you going?' asked Milly.

'To prepare myself. I'm not quite ready to meet Bulkrit yet.'

Milly gave him a puzzled look. Tod was not the same carefree boy she had met by the lake all that time ago. He had changed and seemed a lot more grown up. She would have liked him to explain what he meant, but he turned his back on her and strode purposefully into the Dome.

Sam just shrugged his shoulders and went to tell Red Headband what his men had to do next. He too was worried. He didn't know how long they could control all the Robes or why Tod wanted them all in the Great Hall, but he gripped his armed jetpack firmly and went out to round up the Robes.

The Great Hall was crowded with people. There was a raised platform, like a stage, at the front of the room, and a balcony running all around the sides. Tod had positioned the Waterlanders in a line along this balcony to ensure compliance by the Robes.

Tod made a dramatic entrance. He walked rapidly onto the stage dressed in a new orange robe. But it was no ordinary robe, the edges were lined with white fur and the orange colour was brighter than all the other robes. He held up his hands as a signal for quiet.

The children looked at each other in bewilderment. What on earth was Tod up to?

'I am Tod, son of Ephesus and by right I am the hereditary king of the Robes,' his voice rose to a shout and after a pause he carried on. 'When I was young, my father disappeared and a usurper was made king. Now he has gone and I have returned.' His voice dropped right down to a conciliatory tone and he added, 'Some of you younger ones might remember me?' He looked around the hall expectantly. He had founded and encouraged many of his peer group to join the Society of Young Robes when he had lived in the Dome.

'Toddo!' came a shout from the front and a young Robe raised his hand.

All round the room the cry was taken up. 'Toddo, Toddo' and hands were raised to acknowledge recognition.

Tod nodded with satisfaction. His credentials had been accepted. Bulkrit's face clouded over and he glanced fearfully at the Robes around him. The children stared at Tod in amazement. How could that happy-go-lucky boy have been born a Robe?

Tod looked directly at them and his next words explained what happened. 'I believe my father was murdered and after attempts on my life I realised I had to escape. I swore I would return one day to take up my rightful position. You know the rest of the story. I did find that room in the bottom of the Dome, I was being chased and I was lucky to escape,' he paused to take a breath. 'I knew I could never return to the Dome, so I led a lonely life in the hills, until I met the orphans of Mercy Hall. They took me to a whole new world on the other side of the hedge.' Tod smiled at the children and said softly, 'Thank you for your kindness and I apologise for the deception; it is only since I met the Thinkers, and we found the building of knowledge, that I realised the tremendous future we could have here in the four valleys.'

The hall was a babble of noise, but as soon as Tod held up his arms it went quiet. 'Your leader was Bulkrit, the man I believe to be responsible for the death of my father and the attempts on my life. He will answer to the court of the elders now I am the leader of the Robes.'

Again he paused. 'Who in the ranks of the Robes accepts this decision?' Tod roared out the question and raised his hands in the air.

For a moment there was no response, then the younger ones who remembered Tod, or Toddo, as his friends used to call him, shouted out loudly. 'We do.' Others then took up the call and the response became deafening. When the Robes realised that Tod was destined to lead them anyway, the atmosphere in the hall changed completely. Robes turned to each other and started talking and laughing and shaking hands with each other in sheer delight. The general hubbub carried on for a long time while Tod's face beamed around the hall.

At the back of the hall, the Waterlanders had pushed their way in and Tod took the opportunity to talk to them as well. Again he held up his hands for silence and said, 'In order to use the knowledge left to us by the ancients, I would like the Thinkers and the Waterlanders to join with the Robes to form a united kingdom of the four valleys. I will set up a ruling council here in the Dome.

'What you all need to know now is this: the Waterlanders, the Robes, the Minlings and the Thinkers are all descended from the ancients who lived here many, many years ago.'

Puzzled murmurs filled the hall. Tod continued.

'We have discovered a building in the Thinker's valley. It contains information of a technology far in advance of anything we have here. We will acquire this knowledge and use it to bring us all back together and set us on the next stage of our journey. We were brothers once. We can be brothers again!'

The Thinkers and the Waterlanders and Robes all cheered, leaving the children in no doubt that they would follow Tod in his maddest and craziest venture yet.

Milly looked at Sam and smiled. 'Do you think we underestimated him a little?'

Sam laughed. 'I'll say... We underestimated him completely!'

16

FINAL RETURN

Tod bowed to his audience and left the stage. A lot of excited young Robes were eager to shake his hand, clap him on the back and ask him lots of questions. It was a while before he could free himself and lead the children to a quiet room.

'We had no idea you were a Robe,' said Sam shaking his head, the look of bewilderment still on his face.

'I think you were magnificent out there,' said Singer giving him a big hug.

'Does this mean you are not coming home with us,' asked Milly sadly.

Tod laughed. 'I have learnt so much from all of you. I was amazed at the powers you got from travelling through the Rainbow Cave. Robes were never affected that way. Why should this happen? I don't know.'

'Perhaps somewhere in the books we found there will be an answer,' said Charlie.

'I hope so,' agreed Tod. 'When I spent all that time in the cavern, I realised that there were books and moving pictures that told us how to build and make almost anything. It was amazing! There were instructions on how to make power units like the one that's inside the Dome. And also details of how to rebuild our ship which is, of course, the Dome itself.'

His eyes lit up and a wistful look came on his face. 'There were pictures of other worlds out in space where people moved from planet to planet at speeds we could only dream of.'

'Let's hope they don't all crash when they land!' added Milly, with a smile.

A tick-tock sound alerted everyone to the presence of Batty.

'What about you Batty?' asked Sam, 'Are you staying here or coming home with us?'

Batty had settled on Sam's shoulder and puffed herself up with a fluttery shake. 'I've thought about it, long and hard. There are lots of dangers here - especially for a delicate little thing like me...'

Everyone laughed, never having thought of Batty as delicate.

'However,' continued the bird, 'I do miss old Jangles, and with the Robes not after me any more, I think I'll be quite safe with him. He has promised to look after me.'

'I'm sure he will,' said Sam, giving Batty a gentle stroke down the back. 'But we'll miss you.'

'We had better go home then,' said Milly, biting her lip. 'Robert, George and the rest of the children will be worried.'

Just then, the door burst open and Merfan and Bredon, surrounded by other armed Waterlanders and a few Robes, crowded in. All of them seemed to be in a state of evident agitation.

'When do we go back home to fight the Scarrogs?' asked Bredon, waving a clenched fist.

'How do we move the books in the cavern over here to the Dome?' added Merfan, holding out his empty hands as if expecting the answer to fall into them.

Tod held up his hands and turned to the children. 'See what I mean? If you are returning tomorrow, I'll say goodbye to you then, but right now I have so much to do.' He left the room with the agitated huddle flocking around him, all of them talking at the same time. Bredon was the last to leave the room. As he passed Sam, he held out a small black bag, pressing it into Sam's hand with a firm shake and a sly wink. Sam nodded and stuffed the bag deep into his pocket.

Left alone, the children looked at each other and smiled.

'I think Tod's going to be too busy to think about us for quite a while,' said Charlie.

'Then we'll just have to think for ourselves!' added Milly, placing her hands on her hips. 'It's tomorrow that counts.'

Of course, Tod had thought of his friends. Overnight, he arranged for two of his old Robe friends to accompany them on their journey back to the hedge. They might meet some Robes in the valley of the Minlings who had not heard about the changes at the Dome, so having an escort of Robes would ensure them a safe passage.

There was also a surprise ceremony the next morning before they left.

Merfan stood on the top step by the entrance to the Dome and called out, 'Before you leave, I have to make an award for outstanding bravery to a bird who showed no thought for her own safety and fearlessly attacked Snakeheads as well as travelling on her own through dangerous lands. Batty, I have great pleasure in awarding you 'The Zendoran Medal of the Stars.'

He walked over to where Batty perched on Sam's shoulder and placed a tiny medal, shaped like a star, around her neck. It was made out of gold with a silver chain that sparkled in the light. 'I present this to you with many thanks.' Then he stood back, smiled and clapped his hands. Everyone applauded enthusiastically and Batty opened her eyes wide with surprise. For once in her life, she had nothing to say.

When the short ceremony was over, they bade farewell to all the friends they had made and left the Dome to start their journey home.

Tod walked with them for a while. 'I think we need to keep the hedge closed from now on,' he said with great seriousness. 'I intend to unite all the people here and work to rebuild our ship. After our experiences with Old Barking Mad and the circus people, I think we will be better off staying in our bubble for now.'

The children nodded in agreement. They all

knew this meant their goodbyes were to be for ever, but, as Milly had said, it's tomorrow that counts, so they made their farewells and wished each other the very best of luck. Milly and Singer each gave Tod an extra big hug before they left.

Biting their lips to hold back tears, the children walked quickly to the river where a boat waited to take them through the Rainbow Cave and back to the valley of the Minlings. After all their adventures in this strange land, they were keen to get home.

Once through the cave, Sam held Batty aloft, her medal glinting in the sunlight.

'Well, Batty,' he said. 'Time for you to be off too.'

'Oh yes,' replied the bird. 'Back to Jangles. I shall miss you all.'

'Not as much as we'll miss you,' said Charlie.

'Be good now,' cried the bird, as she launched herself into the air. 'Don't talk to strangers...'

And with her words ringing on the wind, she was gone.

The orphans of Mercy Hall rushed out of the house when they realised the missing children had returned. Everybody wanted to know what had happened behind the hedge and it took the rest of the day for each member of the party to tell their story. Cheer after cheer went up as the events of the journey unfolded, with a particularly loud cheer for Batty, when her story was told, though many were sad they would never see the funny creature again.

Another loud cheer went up when Sam stood up and produced a small bag from his pocket. 'Before we left, Bredon gave me these,' he announced, and poured a glittering pile of precious stones onto the table.

'Diamonds enough to keep us going for a long time yet!'

More cheers rang out, followed by the joyful sounds of excited chatter and much laughter.

It was late into the night when Charlie, Singer, Sam and Milly were left on their own, talking again about their adventures and what they would be doing in the future.

'One day I will write about the land behind the hedge and the strange creatures we found there,' said Charlie.

'No! you can't!' said Milly in alarm. 'It's our big secret. Nobody must ever know about it.'

'Well, with my gift for speaking any sort of language in the world, I will travel, meet all sorts of creatures and write about everything I can.'

'I can't imagine you as a writer of books,' said Singer laughing.

'Just watch me,' said Charlie in a quiet but determined way.

'It's very hard to imagine your name on the cover of a lovely, leather bound book,' said Milly laughing. 'Charlie Trinder, orphan and writer.'

'I shall use a posh name and write epic tales of mystery and adventure, filled with strange creatures from places barely imagined...'

'I can't wait,' said Sam. 'You'd better start right away!'

EPILOGUE

Two years later, Mercy Hall was full of children of all ages and backgrounds. George had left to become articled to a lawyer in Erringford, but the rest of them were still living at the home. Milly had grown taller and heavier but she still had freckles and wore her hair in pig tails.

One morning in early autumn, a robust game of cricket in the grounds was interrupted by an enormous explosion. Everybody stood still and looked around. It came from the direction of the hedge. Over the trees a great bowl of shimmering light rose into the air. Suddenly, it split into thousands of little rainbows and a great domelike shape appeared in the sky. The ground under them started to tremble and some of the younger children screamed in fright. After the explosion, there was a moment's silence, then a rumbling noise started which grew in intensity while the great dome hovered in the air.

'It's the ship,' gasped Charlie. 'I recognise the top of the Dome. They've rebuilt it!' He was standing with Sam, their necks craned upwards to watch the sudden appearance of the massive object. It hovered only for a moment more before jets of flame appeared underneath. Then, with a great rushing sound, it shot straight up into the air like a giant rocket.

The world seemed to stand still as they watched the ship rise steadily higher. The noise quickly diminished and soon there was only the burning tail of a tiny dot to be seen. Moments later it disappeared altogether. Although they all stayed looking at the point where they last saw it, the Dome had gone.

'Look,' said Sam, pointing. 'Look at the hedge.'

All eyes turned to see what had once been a giant and impenetrable hedge slowly sink and crumple to become a quite normal looking tangle of thorns and weeds. Beyond lay a field, pitted and scarred here and there, with a few boulders lying about. A small stream ran through it, disappearing under the largest boulder in the centre of the field.

On top of the boulder sat a bird; quite a normal looking bird, perhaps a starling of some sort. When it saw all the children staring at it, the bird cocked its head slightly to look back at them, puffed up its feathers and chose, quite rightly, not to say a word.

THE END